BROWNING IN BUCKSKIN

Peter Corris was born in Stawell, Victoria, in 1942. From 1964 to 1975 he taught history at Monash, ANU and the University of Melbourne. He has been a professional writer since 1975 and was literary editor of the *National Times* from 1978 to 1980. He lives in Sydney's inner west, works in a city flat and relaxes on the south coast.

BROWNING IN BUCKSKIN

From the tapes and papers
of Richard Browning

transcribed and edited by

Peter Corris

ISBN-10: 0140146997
ISBN-13: 9780140146998

For
JOHN BAXTER

CONTENTS

INTRODUCTION

The fourth volume of Richard Browning's memoirs has required more editorial intervention than previously. Browning was evidently employing a flashback technique when he made these recordings. This is not surprising in one who spent a good deal of his life in the film industry, but Browning was not a reader (see page 133 for his discussion on the matter with Gary Cooper), and he had very little idea of how the technique is best employed in literature. After several taping sessions, he appears to have become aware of this and abandoned the attempt. As a result, the tapes are a jumble of recollections in flashback and in the present time with interpolations that are hard to locate chronologically.

I have endeavoured to present a coherent narrative and, as far as possible, to preserve Browning's notion of how it should be structured, remembering that it was his intention that the memoirs should be published. No decipherable material has been omitted and no words that are not Browning's have been introduced. However, there has been considerable rearrangement.

The enterprise continues to receive generous support from Mr Richard Kelly Featherstone of New York City. Mr Featherstone advises me that he becomes more convinced that Richard Browning was his father as more transcripts become available. He has embarked on his own research into the life of Bonnie Dalton, Browning's lover (see *'Beverly Hills' Browning),* whom he believes to have been his mother. Those interested in Browning's life will await the results of Mr Featherstone's enquiries with keen interest.

Unhappily, others have responded to the publication of the memoirs in less generous ways. I have received letters from three men and two women in the United States and Canada who purport to be Browning's children. Their motives are obvious – to lay claim to any profits that may derive from the sale of these volumes. I am happy to take this opportunity to head off such approaches: any revenue from the books will be used to finance a film based on Richard Browning's life. This seems to be the most appropriate memorial. In the unlikely event that the film makes a profit, this money will be devoted to a charitable purpose which is yet to be determined. No individual can expect to profit.

In this connection, Browning's second, and probably bigamous, marriage to Coral Smith, which is described in this volume, is of particular interest. It is noteworthy that he makes no mention of the possibility of issue from this relationship. Indeed, he expresses satisfaction with the sterility of the next woman he associated with, Glenda Barrow. At this stage of the Browning saga, only two references to children have been made. Browning is alleged to have fathered a child with Katie Ryan, the farmer's daughter with whom he had a brief fling in 1917 (see *'Box Office' Browning,* pp. 56–60,193). His brother-in-law, Rupert MacKnight, made mention of the pregnancy of Browning's first wife, Elizabeth (see *Browning Takes Off,* p. 191). However, both of these references are made in an accusatory and punitive spirit and solid evidence testifying to the existence of any children, legitimate or otherwise is still lacking.

Remarkably little of the considerable volume of mail I have received since the publication of *'Box Office' Browning* offers significant corrections to Dick's testimony. Melbourne broadcaster Terry Lane has pointed out that the Leica camera which Browning claims to have employed in 1919 was not yet in production. Such a slip is excusable in a man of Browning's years and habits, but editorial vigilance should have picked it up. Subsequent editions of the memoirs will make amends on this and other small points of fact.

The work goes on. The tapes are often faint, sometimes incoherent. Increasingly, Browning used the cassettes on which he was recording his memoirs to tape songs he liked from the radio. Consequently, the text is frequently interrupted by snatches of song by such artists as Rudy Vallee, Nelson Eddy, Beniamino Gigli and Al Martino. At one point, preliminary to a recording session, it seems as if Browning is about to burst into song, but he has a drink instead and mutters imprecations about Broadway and Dan Dailey. As there is no evidence that Browning ever considered a career on the stage, the likelihood is that he had hopes of securing a role in the 1948 musical *Give My Regards to Broadway* which starred Dan Dailey. The transcription of further tapes may throw light on this piece of trivia.

Research into this period of Browning's life has been greatly helped by film critic and historian, novelist and scriptwriter John Baxter. Bill Collins, film presenter *extraordinaire* on Network Ten, Australia, and Bob Larkins, writer and researcher attached to the Bill Collins' office, provided invaluable material.

P.C.
Sydney
1991

CHAPTER ONE

Being on the run is no fun. Your clothes stink, your beard itches and your teeth feel as if you've borrowed them from someone else. I should know, I've been in this condition more times than I care to remember. I suppose deserting from the army in 1918 would have been my biggest and riskiest flit, but running out on a pregnant Australian wife four years later and giving myself a permanent discharge from the Canadian Mounties in 1922, have to rate pretty high. In some ways, though, the powder I took in California in 1928 after working for Howard Hughes, having my air transport business stolen from under me and evading a lawsuit brought by my first wife which would have put me in the poorhouse for life,[1] sticks just as horribly in my memory.

I joined a grape-picking gang to get clear of Los Angeles, where my job, friends, money and prospects had evaporated like smoke. Later, I came to understand that life in Hollywood was just like that – constructed of dreams and fantasies on a foundation of flattery (I can't see why David Niven should have a monopoly on this sort of writing; I went through much worse experiences than him) – but then I thought I was the only man in California to suffer terminal bad luck.

Looking back on it now, from a perspective of half a century, I realise that Hollywood *did* tell the truth from time to time. There is one movie that gets it right. Remember Paul Muni in *I am a Fugitive from a Chain Gang*? I saw it a few years after the time I'm talking about and it hit me hard. 'I steal,' Muni hisses at the end when Helen Vinson asks him how he lives. That's right! That's how it was!

I hitched a ride on a hay truck to leave the grape-picking and slept for I don't know how long, waking up itchy and sore (I mean in the English sense of pain, not the American sense of angry, although I was that too) and spoiling for a fight. That is, one I could win. I squinted through the dusty back window of the truck and saw that the driver was a little guy, sucking on a toothpick. A hayseed, pure and simple. I hammered on the glass.

'Stop the truck!' I yelled.

The road was narrow, twisting and rutted. The strip of tar down the middle had been eroded by water, wind and a million wheels. The driver ignored me and his big, red-knuckled hands gripped the steering wheel as if he was propelling the truck with them rather than with his foot on the gas pedal. He kept the left side wheels on the road and let the right side bump along in the dirt. The jolting hurt my hungover head and the dust and crap coming out of the hay bales made me sneeze. What with this and bashing at the glass and swearing, I was exhausted by the time the truck stopped.

'You c'n get down, buddy,' the driver said. 'An' you git no marks for grat'tude at all.'

I climbed down onto the road. As the dust cleared I saw that he wasn't so small after all – maybe a welterweight, and some welterweights have been able to handle light-heavies, which is what I was. Think of Mickey Walker[2]. I concentrated on clearing my throat and rubbing my eyes and let him drive off with his bloody hay to wherever he was going. Bugger him. After *that* cloud of dust had cleared I looked around.

The road straightened out for a mile or so at this point, which is why he'd dropped me here. There couldn't have been any other reason because there was nothing to see – just dried-out fields, tumble-down fences, a few scrubby trees and some blue hills in the far distance. It was one of those roads, and I've been on a few of them in my time, where it made no difference which direction you walked in.

But you walk. I stumbled along the dusty track, vaguely aware that I was heading east because the sun was on my back, and bloody hot it was, too. A few rattletrap pickups travelled the road in the opposite direction. From the grim looks on the drivers' faces I judged that I was going the wrong way in their estimation. No east-bound vehicles appeared. I was light-headed from hunger, thirst and exhaustion when the road suddenly took a bend and a drop and I found myself headed towards a narrow bridge over a struggling creek. *Water,* I thought. *That's good.* Then I saw the buildings; not many, a cluster of shacks with iron roofs, two clapboard stores with skimpy verandahs and one larger structure that looked as if it had actually had a coat of paint since the war. *Civilisation,* I thought. *Maybe even food, drink and tobacco.* You can see that I was starting to feel better from that moment.

Well, Three Cedars was nobody's idea of an oasis. The town consisted of the Three Cedars Auto Camp, the Three Cedars General Store and Pop's Grain Store, Livery Stable & Gas. The general store handled the mail and banking, what there was of it; Pop handled the smashed windscreens, busted axles and liquor, and the auto camp handled the food, laundry and sex. I didn't take all this in at first sight, of course. You'll hardly believe it, but I stayed in that backwater place for almost . . . I guess it must have been a couple of months. Occasionally, I look back on these periods of calm in my life and think they were the good times. Occasionally. A stiff drink usually sets me right.

Some instinct made me turn off the road and make my way down to the settlement. I used the cover afforded by the trees that grew along the side of the creek and a couple of abandoned build-ings that indicated the place had seen better days. I squatted in the creek bed, below the road level, washed my hands and face and took a long drink. I doubt you could find running water anywhere in the

United States that tasted as cool and fresh and pure as Three Cedars creek. It revived, comforted and relaxed me at the same time. I took a long piss in the bushes and lay down with my tired back supported by the grassy bank. God knows I had enough worries on my mind – creditors for sure, a lawyer who'd been robbed of a fee (there's no worse enemy than that) and maybe even the US Immigration Office – but in the clear, warm southern Californian air I fell asleep.

The sun had set when I woke up, and the warmth of the day had gone. I was wearing slacks with rents in the knees, a thin cotton shirt and a blazer which had had a fashionable cut until my recent activities had crumpled it beyond recognition. The blazer was unlined. My shoes were made more for sitting around swimming pools than tramping country roads; my feet inside them and the silk socks were blistered, sore and cold. Worse than the cold was the hunger. I couldn't remember when I'd last eaten, and as soon as I worked out who and where I was – no comfort in either fact – I could think of nothing else except food.

You have to remember that this was California in 1929, it was only about twenty years[3] since Geronimo died for God's sake, and many a man still put a pistol in his pocket right after putting on his hat. You didn't go sneaking around little townships at night. The cemeteries in these towns are full of graves of men shot by trigger-happy citizens. I've seen 'em – the wooden marker usually says 'Stranger' and gives the date of death. Blacks, Chinks and Indians didn't even rate a marker. As I say, you didn't sneak around trying to steal food, not unless you were desperate. I was.

I waited until the lights went out in the windows and then I waited some more before I left the creek bed and crossed the road, bent low. I ducked into the shadows beside a water tank and waited there until I was sure there was nothing moving. After firearms, my biggest worry was dogs, but there's nothing much you can do about dogs and, usually, I had a way with them. Mind you, I've got some tooth scars that say different. There were a couple of dusty cars parked near the auto camp shacks and even one old wagon. I could hear the horse that pulled it chomping on grass in a nearby paddock. Los Angeles was less than thirty miles away but Three Cedars looked to be about thirty years behind it.

Eventually the township was quiet and dark, but there was enough moonlight to see by. I was hoping to find a vegetable patch or an orchard. Sometimes serious drinkers left bottles of beer outside to cool overnight, so they could go to bed and dream of the first good cold one in the morning. The thought of that nearly made my throat seize and I had to stifle a cough.

I moved from the water tank towards the back of the stable cum gas station and drew a blank. The back of the place was a car and farm machinery graveyard that smelt of oil, gas and rotting rubber. I doubt that anything could have grown within a hundred yards of it. Over to the auto camp, scuttling, bent over, all senses alert. I hadn't had a cigarette in twenty-four hours (another thought which produced painful physical sensations) and my sense of smell was sharp. The aroma hit me from fifty yards away. Bread was baking. Yeast was rising, thick crusts were forming. The smell almost drove me mad. I followed my nose and fetched up outside a small brick building at the end of a path that led back to the main section of the auto camp.

I pressed myself flat against the brick wall that seemed warm from the cooking inside. No lights in the cabins. Some washing flapping gently on a clothes line behind the general store. No other movement. I tried the door to the cookhouse and felt the handle turn. I eased the door from the frame, and the smell became richer and more tantalising. Bread, for certain, maybe even pies and biscuits[4]. Butter, perhaps. I opened the door and went inside. The smells were overpowering; it was like having gone without sex for a year and suddenly finding yourself inside a French brothel. I had to take the risk. I fumbled a box of matches from my pocket and lit one. In its flickering light I saw the ovens and the loaves that were sitting on top of them. I could see a big butter pot and jars of preserves and chutneys.

I lit another match and marked where everything I wanted was. Then, in the darkness I snatched a loaf, dug a hole in it and shoved in a fistful of butter. I took a jar of preserves and cramed it into my blazer pocket, ripping the stitching. There was nothing to drink but I had the creek. I crammed the hunk of warm bread I pulled out into my mouth and stepped through the door.

The lantern beam hit me in the eyes, blinding me. I guess I blinked, I know I kept on chewing because I could feel the crumbs and suddenly-released saliva dripping down my chin.

'You sure are a messy eater.'

A woman's voice. Relief flooded through me.

'I can explain,' I said through a mouthful of bread.

'Stop right there, mister! This is a twelve gauge, double barrel.'

I squinted, raised my free hand and tried to shield myself from the unwavering light. I saw the business end of a shotgun centered on my chest. Instinctively, I covered the spot with the loaf of bread. This drew an amused snort.

'That won't save you.'

Young or old? I thought desperately. *How do I look? Probably terrible, but surely not dangerous. If only I can swallow the bread I can smile. That'll give me a chance.* I chewed and gasped for breath.

'You're the hungriest dead man I ever saw.'

The voice was youngish, I was sure of it. I got the bread down and flashed the famous Browning choppers. 'Madam, I want to apologise . . .'

There was a roar and a spurting flame. I felt red hot needles pierce my body and then everything went black. I tried to hang onto the loaf of bread but it weighed a ton and was pushing me down to the cold, hard ground.

CHAPTER TWO

I woke up in a soft, clean bed in a warm, dry room. A woman was sitting in a chair by the bed. At first I thought it was my mother, then I recognised her. I lifted my head from the pillow with a sharp jerk that sent pinpricks of pain through my body. I sank back and would have moaned if my throat hadn't been so dry. She poured a glass of water from a jug on the bedside table. Her hands were strong and comforting as she lifted my head and supported it while I drank. The water oiled the voice box.

'You shot me!'

'Bird shot,' she said. 'Hardly touched you. I picked the lead out of your legs while you were in your faint.'

I closed my eyes. It was a relief to know I still had my legs and other accessories; her tone was a bit hard to take though. 'I was exhausted. Starving. I've been ill. I . . .'

She took a flask of pale amber fluid from the pocket of her dress, poured a measure into the glass and added the same amount of water. Suddenly I wanted that drink more than my pride or my manhood or anything else. She read the message in my eyes.

'Just you have a little drink of this here and get back to sleep. We'll talk some in the morning. My, the way you got that bread down.' A smile spread across her face making it almost pretty. Without the smile it was what you'd call strong, if you 'were being kind. Want something to eat?'

I lifted my head for the drink and took it down in a couple of long gulps. The whisky warmed and soothed my mouth, throat, belly, every part of me. It was like a warm oil massage from the inside out. I smiled as she lowered my head. 'No, thank you, Ma'm.'

'I like a polite man. We'll get along fine.' She rose and moved to the door. I could see that she was medium-sized with thick dark hair tied back. She wore a plain blue dress with a light shawl around her shoulders. Pretty good body from the waist up; I resisted the impulse to lift my head and get a look at her legs.

I raised my hand from the counterpane in a gesture of gratitude plus courtliness. I'd seen Doug Fairbanks do it many times and it always seemed to have the right effect. She smiled again and closed the door. I lay back thinking, *Dick, old man, I'd say you've fallen on your feet here.*

Her name was Coral Smith although she'd been Coral Canetti for three years while she was married to the Italian who'd owned the joint. Canetti had died of pneumonia eight months back and Coral had resumed her maiden name as soon as she decently could. The sign outside still read 'L. Canetti prop.' under 'Auto Camp & Diner'.

'How come you married him?' I asked Coral. This was over lunch two days after she shot me. Since then she'd been feeding me like a prince and keeping me well topped up with the best moonshine whisky I ever drank. I'd seen a photo of Canetti on the living room dresser – all handlebar moustaches and moist, dumb eyes.

Coral heaped more fried potatoes onto my plate. 'You'd been through what I had, Nick, you wouldn't ask that question.' She took a small sip of wine – the Italian had laid in some pretty good red – and gave a grin. 'Hell, *you'd* have married him.'

That was Coral, she'd shift from grim to light-hearted in a second. I found it very likeable. We shared a laugh about me marrying Canetti, and I got across the information to her that I wasn't married, which may or may not have been true. God knows what

Elizabeth MacKnight-Browning was up to in Australia. I'd also told her that my name was Nick Brown which sounded close enough to the real thing to make me comfortable.

'Smith 'n Brown,' she'd said when I told her this. 'Couple of ordinary folks.'

We'd laughed at that too. You can see that we were getting along like a house on fire, had done in fact, from the first time I sat up in bed and really paid attention to her and the place I'd landed in. Coral was about thirty years old, a bit younger than me but I told her it was the other way around and she believed me. She was a very smart woman. She didn't owe any money on the establishment and she was making it pay. The diner did good business at weekends and mid-week and the cabins were usually fully occupied (I'd arrived on a quiet night.) This wasn't just because the beds were clean, a rarity in backwoods hostelries in those days I can tell you, or that the food was good. Canetti's was the place men from miles around took women and where women from miles around took men. The police did it and several judges, so the place had protection.

Coral liked to cook. She had a Mexican woman to help her, but she did a lot of the cleaning work herself. I asked her why.

'On account of people leave things behind, careless like. Letters, jewellery and such.'

'You blackmail them?'

'No, I don't, an' they know it. That's why they come to my place and keep coming.'

As I say, she was smart, but so am I, and I had her eating out of my hand after a day or two. I played the invalid, claimed loss of memory, had small relapses and had to take to my bed, often. She was busy from morning to night, but she kept making small visits (I kept well out of sight of the customers for reasons of decorum) to bring me coffee, cigarettes and magazines.

On the third night I let her give me a bath. I kept myself decently under the suds, but she saw the set of my shoulders and seemed to enjoy soaping up and rinsing out my thick hair. I guess she'd already seen other things when she picked the birdshot out of my legs. Nothing happened then. I towelled off and went to bed early in her spare room with a stiff whisky for company. I could hear her moving restlessly around in the house. I got up early, but not before her, and went to the wash-house for a clean-up and a shave. I shaved close, brushed my hair and put on a clean shirt. I refused breakfast and just had a cup of coffee. She asked if I felt all right. I was non-committal. I stayed in my room throughout the early morning. I heard her giving detailed instructions to the Mexican woman about what she wanted done around the place.

The door opened sometime around 11 a.m. She was carrying a tray with a coffee pot, a whisky flask and some cookies on it. She'd taken some trouble with her hair; it was glowing from the brush and tied with a bright ribbon. She'd put on some lipstick and changed out of her working dress into a soft, slightly frilly affair with a scooped out neck. She put the tray down on the bed and sat carefully beside it. The tray was between us; we were a couple of feet apart.

'Thought you might like a pick-me-up, Nick. Coffee and a shot?'

I nodded. She poured two coffees and added the moonshine. I reached for the cup and our hands touched. Her hands had done a lot of work but she'd rubbed some sort of cream into them to make them softer and her nails were freshly trimmed. She was wearing perfume and she didn't smell of tobacco which was unusual because she was almost as heavy a smoker as me. We drank our laced coffee and didn't speak. A man and a woman sitting on a bed. A man and a woman saying nothing but silently signalling what was on their minds.

'Things'll be pretty quiet today,' she said. 'Being Monday. Maria knows what to do.'

'You work hard, Coral,' I said.

'Always have, but work isn't everything, is it?'

I finished my coffee. Good coffee and good whisky go together like satin and lace. I was warmed through and relaxed. Time to make a move. I put my cup on the tray, took hers and put it on top of mine. Then I shifted the tray to the chest of drawers which was a long stretch but I made it pretty elegantly. I winced though as I set the tray down.

'Where does it hurt, Nick?'

'It doesn't hurt.' I reached for her and she came into my arms like a wife greeting a husband back from the war. I stroked her hair and kissed her ear and did several other safe things before I put a hand inside her dress and touched somewhere that mattered. After that, it all went pretty much as you'd expect. She was no blushing virgin and I'd been screwing women of all shapes and sizes, in a dozen different countries, for more than twenty years. One point of interest was that it had evidently been lean pickings for both of us for some time past and we were keen as mustard. I don't know how many times we did it in that one session, but I remember being topside and below decks more than once and we weren't always on the bed. In fact we tore the room apart, spilt the coffee and ended up on the floor sharing a cigarette and the whisky flask and laughing like idiots.

'God, my legs!'

There were bloody spots oozing through the bandages. *Time to get this thing into the right perspective,* I thought. I let her help me back onto the bed. She tidied herself, then she cleaned up the room and fetched more whisky and coffee. She kissed me so hard I had to fight for breath and then she went back to managing her lucrative little business. I settled down onto the pillows and felt all my cares float away. Well, that's paradise, isn't it – a woman who fucks like the Queen of Sheba, works like a navvy, cooks well, takes a drink and earns enough for two to live on? I was willing to bet I was the first Browning in history to find one. I know that my Dad, 'Wild Bill', missed out on all scores.

I never meant to stay in Three Cedars but, looking back, I can see why I did. It was September 1929 when I arrived and everyone knows what happened the following month. The stock market crash hit America like a bomb, and I wasn't the only man with a safe billet who hunkered down and stayed put. After all, what did I know about earning a living in America? Flying planes and acting in movies – neither seemed like a safe bet in October 1929. Added to that, there was Coral. Once the ice between us was broken there was no stopping her: she treated me like a king through the day and like a sultan at night.

I did a little work around the place – mended a few fences, painted the cabins, kept Coral's 1927 Cadillac La Salle in working order. But mostly my job was to sit in the diner, read the newspaper, smoke a cigar and chat to the customers. It wasn't always easy; some of them were tough cops from LA and the border towns who were naturally suspicious of a 'sweetback man'[5] like me. The politicians and other grafters on the public payroll understood me better, but they were dull company. One thing everyone agreed on was that times were bad and likely to get worse.

'Got any investments, Mr Brown?' one of the customers, a drummer for pharmaceutical products, asked me.

I shook my head. 'Not a one. My big business reverse happened before the crash. My partners gypped me out of everything.' I'd told Coral a version of the story of how 'Bluey' Tait and Terri Driver had robbed me, keeping the details vague. She was listening to this conversation and she gave me a sympathetic glance while I tried to look like a man who was planning a comeback.

The drummer folded the paper he'd been reading and lit a cigarette. 'Well, think of it this way. If they put any of the money they took from you into stock, chances are they're as broke as you are now.'

I tried the idea out and liked it. Coral thought the smile I gave was for her; she came across and put her strong right arm around my shoulders. 'Nick's not broke,' she said. 'He's got the best investment in the world.'

Later that night, after a solid supper of spare ribs and chilli and a couple of pitchers of beer which had put us in the mood for some energetic love-making, I asked her what she meant.

'I meant me, dummy.' We were on the big brass bed in her room, both naked as new-born babes; somehow I'd got one of her stockings wound around my neck. She gave the end a tug. 'There's not a penny owing on this place, and you know what it makes a week. Taxes're low and people're going to eat and make love right up to the crack o' doom.'

'That's true. But I don't see . . .'

She shut me up with a deep hungry kiss and we got back into it all over again. I found myself thinking of various things as she plunged and bucked her way to a climax. I'd told her I was twenty-six years old and an Englishman of good family – only slight exaggerations there – also that I was single and childless, which was true for all practical purposes. I'd also said that I had no money which was the honest truth.

'Do you love me, Nick?'

After what she'd just finished doing to me only an absolute oaf could have replied in the negative. 'Of course I do.'

'Well, let's get married. Then half of everything I've got'll be yours.'

CHAPTER THREE

I should have smelled a rat right there and then, but I've never been one to look a gift horse in the mouth and Coral was an amiable woman quite apart from her other qualities. And of course I'd be marrying her under a false name with scarcely an accurate word on the documents, so it didn't feel like a binding contract to me. I showed a little hesitation at first which only made her try all the harder to please me. When I agreed she was over the moon.

'We'll honeymoon in Hollywood, Nick. What do you say?'

'Ah, . . . bit cheap, Hollywood, I've always thought. Wouldn't New Orleans be more romantic?'

She gave me one of her deep, smacking kisses. 'By God, you're right! What a man. Nawlins'd have to be the most romantic city in America.'

So, we went ahead with it. On 1 December, 1929, Nicholas Richard Brown, bachelor, business executive, born Tunbridge Wells, England, 10/3/02, married Coral Canetti, nee Smith, widow, cafe proprietor, born Denver, Colorado, 11/11/99. It was one of the smaller and quieter of my weddings – just a few of the customers at the chapel in Red Springs, which was the nearest town with a church, and a few drinks and a barbecue back home. I went to bed drunk which, come to think of it, has been a feature of marriage nights as I've experienced them.

Through her police contacts Coral fixed me up with a driver's licence so I could share the driving to Louisiana. We couldn't leave on the honeymoon right away because the Red Springs' rodeo was on which made for a couple of busy days in Three Cedars. I was in the diner two nights before we were due to leave when Walter MacMurray walked in and sat at my table.

'Nick, congratulations.' MacMurray extended his big hand and we shook. 'Fine woman.'

'Yes, she is. Thank you.' MacMurray had been through a couple of times in the past few weeks. He was a tall, strongly built man with thick, black hair and a squarish jaw. He looked as if he could handle himself which, of course, made me wary of him. He had a bluff, not over-friendly manner, which surprised me because his job was selling insurance. From my days in the wine business in Australia and aviation and acting in America, I was accustomed to a much oilier type in that line of work. MacMurray used to come in, have a meal, read through some business papers and drive off. Once, I think, he stayed overnight in the auto camp, but it was a night I really tied one on and I don't remember much about it.

He reached into his briefcase, took out some papers and put them on the table in front of me. Then he unscrewed the top of his fountain pen.

'What's this?' I said.

'Your wife's idea. I just had a word with her. She thinks you two should both take out insurance policies.'

I lit a cigarette to give myself time to think. *Insurance? Didn't that mean birth certificates, medical examinations, life histories?* 'First I've heard of it. I don't know . . .'

'Simple life policy. Ten thousand dollar cover. Nothing to it, just to protect the business in case something should happen. Later, when the kids come along, well, we'd have to take another look.'

'I'm, ah . . . looking around for a business opening. I don't know if I can manage the premiums just yet.'

'Mrs Brown says the business can pay the premiums. That's above board, lots of my clients do that.'

'Surely there's a medical examination? You might have heard that I've been unwell. On the mend now, of course. We're off in a day or two, bound to help the recovery. Perhaps when we come back.'

MacMurray waved his pen and winked. 'Doc Parsons from Red Springs has vouched for your health and vitality. I've got his certificate right here.'

'I've never met the man.'

MacMurray let out a bellow of laughter. 'He's met you. Helped you to bed on your wedding night. Said he never saw a fitter man, nor a drunker one.'

I smiled weakly. 'Surely that's a bit casual for your purposes. What company do you represent, Walter?'

'Western American. They pride themselves on a folksy, no red tape approach. If Doc Parsons says you're healthy, that's good enough. Besides, Coral wouldn't marry a man who wasn't in the prime of condition.'

'What the hell do you mean by that?'

'No offence, Nick, no offence. Just our American way of putting things. I guess you do everything more formally over in England.'

I nodded. I didn't want to get into any discussions about England where I hadn't set foot in ten years. Anyway, I couldn't see any major objection. I wasn't planning to stay longer than I had to, probably just as long as Coral's energetic and imaginative brand of love-making held my interest. If our names on a couple of insurance policies made her happier, who was I to deny her the pleasure? MacMurray showed me Coral's signature under the stipulation that I was the beneficiary in the event of her death. The answers on my section of the policy paper had been written in which was fine by me, I've always found filling out forms a terrible bore. I skimmed a few of the clauses without much interest – it was all to do with a person who didn't exist anyway – and signed with a flourish.

MacMurray gave me his hand to shake again.

'Have a nice honeymoon.'

The honeymoon was a roaring success. We drove clean across the south-west and the La Salle never missed a beat. I've always enjoyed driving good cars, and this was a beauty. Coral was as enthusiatic a bed partner in San Antonio after a hot day on the road as she was in Houston after a day lying around the swimming pool. In the Beauregard Hotel on Bourbon Street in New Orleans, there was no stopping her. She dressed up in yellow silk with feathers and black lace gloves like a French whore, and she played the part right down to the encore.

I admit I spent most of the time in a haze of sex, French champagne, fine food and Cuban cigars. We must have eaten in twenty different restaurants in two weeks – high-class French places that served frogs' legs and quail, speakeasies that specialised in rare hamburgers, and Cajun dives with gumbo that stuck to the roof of your mouth and burned all the way down and out the other end. Coral paid for everything; she was far and away the most generous of my wives.

The night before we left we went to the boxing at the Polo Grounds and I saw a different side of Coral. Sure, she got a bit loud after a few drinks and liked to dance, even sing a little, but she wasn't what you'd call a naturally wild woman. Not like some I've known, such as Clara Bow and Belinda Douglas[6], who could keep drinking, dancing, singing and screwing for days on end. We were a little high when we took our ringside seats. The first fight was a slow affair between a couple of tired middleweights who looked like hangovers from the toe-the-line days. Les Darcy could have put them both to sleep inside a minute. I said so to Coral.

She yawned. 'Who?'

'Les Darcy. He was a great fighter. From Australia.'

'Where?'

You can see that I sometimes had difficulty getting a good chinwag going with Coral. But she was sharp, and if I'd waxed knowledgeable about Australia she'd have suspected something. It's often

like that, I've found, when you're going under a false identity –
conversation gets inhibited. So I shut up and tried to take an interest in two skinny featherweights who had about the same amount
of skill and consequently didn't lay a glove on each other. I felt
Coral's interest stir when the main event fighters got into the ring
– a chunky, barrel-chested bruiser named 'Sailor' Jones and a tall
negro called 'Honey' Clinton. The contest was called a heavyweight
bout, and the Sailor might have scaled two hundred pounds, mostly
in the shoulders and thighs, but if Honey was more than a hundred
and eighty ringing wet I was a Dutchman.

After the introductions – both of them were the heavyweight
champions of somewhere or other – they went at it as if they meant
it. Sailor was a rusher who specialised in roundhouse clubbing
punches. The only defence he knew was a crouch which, admittedly,
did make it difficult for a taller man to hit him anywhere except
the top of the head. Honey was cute; he danced, speared in jabs and
light crosses and seemed to be almost counting the points he was
tallying up. The first round was brisk and a nice mixture of brawn
and science. Everyone was happy.

Coral was ecstatic. 'He's great,' she gasped. 'See the way he
moves. Like a dancer. And I'll bet those punches sting.'

'He won't know what hit him if Jones connects,' I grunted.
'He's giving away more than twenty pounds.'

Coral was on the edge of her seat. 'Let's see. Here we go.'

The bell rang and the pattern of the first round was repeated –
rush and swing, dance and jab. Sailor caught the negro on the ribs;
the smack of the punch was like a pistol shot.

'Cracked ribs,' I said. 'He's gone.'

'No!' Coral yelped. 'No, he's not!'

She was right. Honey Clinton tucked his right arm in over the
ribs, kept the fist cocked but protective, and jabbed the Sailor silly
with his left. The crowd was on its feet at the end of the round
because it looked as if the Sailor might go down like someone stung

by a hundred bees. But he stayed upright, staggered to his corner and spat blood into the bucket.

Coral jabbed me in the ribs. 'Who's got who now, huh? Wise guy. Wanna little bet?'

That was when I first noticed the looks. A few glances only, from the seats on either side, eyeing Coral in her yellow silk, and me, sweating somewhat, in grey flannel. A few words were said, but I couldn't catch them. I wasn't paying that much attention; I was too interested in the fight.

Clinton decked the Sailor with a left hook in the third. It wasn't a hard punch, but it was classically timed to catch the heavier, slower man off balance. Jones went down with a thud and a rush of air from his tense, surprised body.

Coral jumped to her feet. 'Kill 'im!' she screamed. 'Go in an' kill 'im!'

I heard hostility all around, expressed in the clinking of money, low curses, angry puffs on cigars and cigarettes, and then it hit me. There were a lot of negroes in the stadium, maybe a third of the audience was black, but there were none at ringside. The only black men within fifty feet of us were Honey and his two corner men. I glanced around and saw that blacks and whites were seated in separate sections further back and above. Coral was one of about a dozen white women close to the ring. She was the only white person cheering for Honey Clinton. I pulled her back onto her seat.

'Shut up,' I hissed. 'You're in the south, and you're cheering for a darkie.'

'I don't give a damn,' she said. 'Twenty bucks on Honey. Any takers?'

A fat man in a white suit sitting in the row in front turned around slowly and looked at me with sagging, bloodhound eyes. 'If'n you can't keep her quiet, son,' he drawled, 'I think y'all better leave.'

'I'm not leavin'!' Coral yelled, but the bell and an explosion of action in the ring drowned her out. The Sailor rushed across the canvas apparently determined to end things quickly. Blood spurted from his mouth as he started his first punch, a looping right delivered from an almost erect stance. The negro swayed back, perfectly balanced, and made the Sailor miss; he took a small step forward and let go the right he'd kept cocked since he'd been hit in the ribs. It was one of those moments at a fight when you see everything very clearly and in slow motion. I could see the agony on Honey's face as he threw the punch; the pain from the ribs must have been incredible. But he threw it and with all his weight behind it. Sailor was like a buffalo running smack into a .303 bullet. The punch connected with his upthrust jaw, and you could almost see the message travel along the bone to his brain. His legs crumpled and he pitched forward onto his face. Honey had to skip out of his way to give him room to fall.

'Whoopee,' Coral screamed. 'Whatta punch!'

There was a lot of noise in the crowd among the blacks, who were cheering their man and slapping each other on the back and showing each other exactly what the sweet moves had been. Things were pretty quiet at ringside. They lifted the Sailor off the floor and got him moving in a minute or so by using smelling salts. He got a bit of a cheer as he left the ring, heavily supported by his handlers. Honey Clinton lifted the ropes fastidiously and stepped through them.

'Yes, sir,' Coral yelled. 'Honey is sweet!'

A man sitting a few places along from me spat tobacco juice on the sawdust-covered floor. He stood, leaned across and shoved his face close to mine. His breath stank like a swamp, and his voice had a whine like a power saw stuck in hardwood. 'Mistuh, I wouldn't keep a woman like that in the backyard on a chain.'

The colour drained from Coral's face as she looked at me. I looked at the man; he was shorter than me and a good deal lighter. I took a chance and threw a left hook at his stubbly chin.

All hell broke loose at ringside; men started punching and shoving and women were screaming and clawing. One woman flew at Coral with her hands out like talons. Coral yanked at her hair and swung her around like a mop in a bucket. I was hit in the stomach by the tobacco juice spitter and went down. I took a boot in the head and almost lost interest in the proceedings. I could hear words like 'nigger' and 'coon' being shouted, and there was the sound of clothing being torn and fists smacking into faces. I don't know how I got out, Coral must have helped, but eventually I found myself outside the stadium in the heavy, moist, scent-laden air.

'Can you walk, Nick, honey?' Coral said.

'I guess so.' I wobbled for a few steps until I got the hang of it. 'What happened?'

Coral chuckled. In the streetlight I could see that her dress was torn, and some white flesh and oyster pink satin were showing. It was the sort of thing that usually made an impact on me, but just then I wasn't in the mood. Whistles were blowing and car engines were roaring. 'Isn't it exciting,' Coral said. 'Three Cedars is going to seem a mite dull after this.' She supported me as we turned away from the commotion and made off down a street where the lamplight shone brightly through thick clusters of frangipani.

'Coral, what happened?'

'Didn't you see? Some 'a those people around the ring weren't white at all. They were light-coloured. What do they call the women?'

'High yellers,' I said.

'Right. High yellers. You know what I did, Nick? I started a race riot!'[7]

CHAPTER FOUR

For someone with capital, there were a lot of business opportunities in New Orleans after the crash. Saloons, cafes and even small hotels were going pretty cheap, and Coral, with experience in these lines of work, plus her ability to run a low-key whorehouse, could have made a killing. I tried to persuade her to sell Three Cedars and make the move.

'No chance, honey. There's no one there with money to buy.'

'Come on,' I said, 'Judge Brennan could buy you out with his small change, and some of those San Diego cops must be looking for investments.'

She had no answer to that, but she wouldn't budge.

I made a last try after she'd paid the bill – a pretty hefty one it was too – and we were loading up the car. You see, I reckoned that the width of the American continent between me and my first wife's legal representatives was about the right distance. A little adjustment northwards wouldn't have hurt either. 'Let's point this thing north, Coral,' I said.

'What?'

She was wearing a smart travelling dress, a little tight over her bottom, which had spread a bit as a result of the good living. I gave her rump a friendly pat. 'I've got a yen to see New York. Let's take a trip up there now, look around a bit. You might feel different about going back to Three Cedars after you've seen New York. I hear they're going to put a building there more than a hundred stories high.'[8]

Coral twitched away from my slap. She snatched the keys from me, marched around the car and got in behind the wheel. '*I'm* goin' back to Three Cedars,' she said. 'You can go to New York if you like. Send me a postcard, if you can raise the price of a stamp.'

Well, put like that, what could I do? I got in beside her and we started back west. I have to say that she was her usual good-natured self within a mile or two, but I never felt quite the same about her after seeing her yelling for blood at ringside and that snappish exchange. I began to wonder about her background as the Caddy ate up the miles. The stuff about me on the marriage licence was a pack of lies: what about nee Smith, Denver, Colorado, and the rest of it? I resolved to do a little digging when we got back to California.

The trip back was quieter than the one across. We had a few crates of champagne and some good liquor aboard, but somehow we didn't seem to be in the mood for it, and we mostly drank beer in the places we stopped. We made love pretty energetically but less often. We listened to the radio a lot – the Minstrels, Bing Crosby, Rudy Vallee . . . [Browning hums tunelessly at this point. I have played the tape to experts on the popular music of the period, but they have been unable to identify the melody. Ed.] Truth is, we both had things on our minds.

Nothing had changed in Three Cedars except that the weather had got a little colder. Pop's grain store still turned out the best bootleg whisky in the state; the general store acted as a drop for the dirty money that changed hands in the county and, well, you know what went on at the auto camp. It wasn't quite a closed system; the road through the town branched and went north to the southern reaches of the Grand Canyon and south to El Paso in Texas, where everything and everybody was for sale. Both places were holes in the ground as far as I was concerned, but there was some interesting through traffic. Sitting in the diner, I met stockbrokers on their way to Mexico; high-class whores headed in the same direction for abortions (sometimes these two categories linked up); virginal couples on their way to honeymoon at Lake San Carlos and trekkers planning to walk the length of the canyon.

They had stories to tell about other places and often left newspapers behind. I learned from an LA paper that *Hell's Angels* had finally been finished early in the new year, and that it was due for release in about six months. There was no movie house in Three Cedars. None of the residents would see me defying death in the air for a year at least. The economy was in collapse, and it looked like Schmelling was going to fight Sharkey.

Most of the travellers were too wrapped up in their own affairs to be curious about me, but one evening I got a fright. I'd been holding forth on some subject or other, wine perhaps, when this English accent stopped the flow.

'I say, Mr Brown, what d'you think of this chap Bradman?'

Bow-tie, hornrims, tweed jacket and as English as a pork pie. Not worth worrying about. I shrugged and said, 'Who?'

'Bradman, the Australian batsman. You're Australian, aren't you? They're expecting great things from him in England this summer.'

The two or three other people around the table didn't know what he was talking about so they looked to me for a response. I cleared my throat; normally I fancied I spoke with a sort of mid-Atlantic accent, a bit like, though I hate to admit it, Errol Flynn's. Now I tried to give it as much Californian flavour as I could. 'Spent a bit 'a time there – when I was a young 'un.'

'Really. I'm a student of languages, accents, that sort of thing. I'd have said . . .'

'The gentleman's talking about cricket, boys,' I said hastily. 'It's a game they play in the rain in England.'

I got a bit of a laugh with that and a few more when I explained the rules of cricket. The Englishman took himself off in a huff and the moment passed. But you can see how careful a thorough-going liar has to be. It's hard work.

I've never played much cricket or followed it very closely. There was the time when David Niven blackmailed me into a match. That bastard Flynn was in on it. . . [The recording on this tape ends here. It is possible that Browning continued with this anecdote on another tape and put it in chronological sequence. In any event, the next cassette resumes where he left off. Ed.]

By and large though, I've always enjoyed the sort of one-off meetings I had with folks in the diner. It's the people who hang around or come back later to screw you that worry me. Anyway, I spent a pleasant few weeks back at Three Cedars. I drove the La Salle around the back roads, saying I was looking for property investments, but really just enjoying the speed and handling of the car. I did a little hunting in the woods with an old .22 rifle I found around the place and bringing home neatly drilled rabbits boosted my prestige. I was well fed by day, tucked up warm with Coral at night and looking for a way to put together a travelling stake when the time came to move on. The most promising course of action was to put the squeeze on one of the public notables who came to the auto camp to play around. It wouldn't have been too hard to get a photograph or perhaps a cashed check, something of the kind. The trouble was, I lacked the nerve to do it.

One night, maybe six weeks into the new year, Walter MacMurray blew into town. He took a shack for the night and came into the diner for a meal. He out-talked, out-ate, out-drank and outstayed everyone else in the place. I was feeling bored and restless by this time and I kept pace with him, at least as far as the drinking was concerned. Coral went to bed leaving me to close up. Walter opened another bottle and poured a big slug for us both. We were the best of pals by this time.

'Nick, ol' buddy, I c'n see you got plenty on your mind.'

'Don't know about that,' I said. 'Like what?'

Walter winked. 'Bottoms up. You're fixin' to leave, but you don't know how.'

I glanced around sharply to make sure that the door to our living quarters was closed. No, it probably wasn't a sharp glance, more of a slow, unfocussed stare. 'What're you talking about, Walter?'

'Life,' MacMurray said. 'You're a young man, an' you're trapped here in this nowhere town.'

'Gotta wife,' I muttered. 'House . . .'

'Her house, not yours.'

'Well . . .'

'Lissen,' MacMurray put his arm over my shoulders and pulled my ear close to his face. 'I'm not a bad guy, Nick.'

I tried to pull away. 'No, no, of course not.'

'Never did anything like this before, but I need the dough.'

'Dough? Did what? I don't understand.'

'How would you like to collect on that insurance policy?'

'Collect? I'd have to be dead, ten thousand's no good to me dead.'

'Twenty thousand, fifteen for you, five for me.'

'Eh?'

MacMurray finished his drink. I drank too, although I was already pretty drunk. Trouble was, I could feel sobriety wrapping itself around me like a cold, wet sheet. He chuckled as he refilled the glasses. 'Put one over on little ol' Coral there. Signed you up for twenty grand without her noticing.'

'Oh.' The thought that I was worth twenty thousand dead and not twenty cents alive almost completed the sobering process.

"S right. Gotta play all the angles in this game. All over the country there's people insured for they don't know how much. Some of 'em don't even know they's insured at all.'

'Very careless,' I said.

'Yep. Now ol' Walt Mac, he's not careless. No, sir. He's careful. Very careful an'. . .'

I was pretending to be drunker than I was by now. I prodded him in the chest and was surprised to feel the hard muscle and sinew stretched over the bone. 'Then how come you need dough, like you say you do?'

MacMurray sighed. 'Woman trouble. Story of my life. Jus' between you 'n me, I got a wife in Texas an' one in California an' damn me if they didn't get together an' hire themselves a hot-shot Jew lawyer. If I can't come up with ten grand real quick I'm gonna be eatin' tortillas for the rest of my life or rotting in gaol.'

'You said you'd get five thousand.'

He grinned, thinking, I'll bet, that he had me. 'I got five, Nick; I need another five to make ten.'

What I've learned, over a long, disreputable life, is that con men love to talk. It's how they make their living, and when they're with a mark who doesn't know what's going on, they can weave a magic spell with their tongues. But if you suspect them from the start, and *then* let them talk, why, it's child's play to see through their scheme and avoid it. (The trouble is, in my case, I've been on both sides of the fence, and I've let myself run off at the mouth and see the scepticism cloud over people's eyes. . .) Anyway, that night in Three Cedars, I let MacMurray talk.

'Everyone knows you drive that Caddy like a bat out a' hell, Nick. Right?'

I shrugged. It's essential to keep as quiet as possible yourself in this manoeuvre.

'Roads round here'r bad. Wouldn't surprise anyone if you 'n it was found wrapped round a tree one day.'

'Guess not.'

'Damn right. Now it so happens I've been writing policies for a company that's building a bridge an' highway south of here. Maybe you know about it?'

I did. I'd driven in that direction and seen the massive construction – a span across a deep ravine and half a mountain being blasted away to allow a road to go directly west instead of looping fifty miles south. I nodded.

'Between you 'n me and this bottle, I can tell you that they're hiring any riff-raff that comes along on that job, and there's some riff-raff around, believe me. City guys, men who've never worked construction before, rummies, guys a shingle short of a roof, know what I mean?'

'Sure, but . . .'

'They're dying, Nick. Dying steady – they're falling, getting blown up, being run over. Violent deaths. We're trying to work out an accident insurance plan, but it's hard to do on account of the work conditions're so piss-poor.'

'I still don't see what it's got to do with me.'

'Look, some of those bodies aren't getting all the care and attention you'd wish for your grey-haired mother. See?'

'No.'

'Don't be dumb. They're dumping them. Hiding them. I guarantee that within a week I could come up with a dead white male, 'bout your size and age, no questions asked.'

I stared at him. 'You mean . . . ?'

'Caught on at last? I knew you would. You're not what you make yourself out to be, Nick. For one thing, you're not no twenty-eight-year-old. I got experience at these things and if you're not thirty-three or thirty-four, I'm a virgin. I've seen you clean your shoes and handle a rifle. You were in the service. Maybe the British army, maybe not, but you're not a limey. I heard talk about a professor was through here. Reckoned you was from South Africa or some such place. I don't think Coral'd take too kindly to being deceived like that. Women got their strange pride, y'know.'

I poured another big drink and didn't say anything.

'No skin off my ass, buddy. We guys who live by our wits gotta stick together. Here's the deal – you keep driving the La Salle the way you do, maybe bang her up a little. I get hold of a John Doe. The car hits a tree and burns with John Doe inside. Doc Parsons identifies you. You hide out someplace. American Western pays off and we all collect.'

'How? Coral'd get the money.'

'Sure she'd get it. Then you turn up alive. You figure she's going to give it back? No chance. It's hers which means it's yours, and some of it's mine. 'Course you'd have to get away from here, but that wouldn't be a big problem would it, Nick?'

I shook my head and drained the glass.

'So, whaddya say?'

I swayed in my chair, let my head wag loosely from side to side and collapsed forward onto the table. 'Think about it,' I said. Then I let go a long, paint-stripping snore.

CHAPTER FIVE

Of course, I didn't believe a word of MacMurray's plan. I pretended to sleep across the table, while he smoked another cigarette and finished his drink. I could sense that he wasn't nearly as drunk as he'd pretended to be – that made two of us. After he'd gone off to his shack, I washed my face, made a pot of coffee and sat drinking it and smoking while I thought things out. It wasn't too hard to figure – I remembered the night MacMurray had stayed over while I passed out drunk. Ten to one on he'd slept with Coral. And there was her unwillingness to even consider not coming back to Three Cedars. The question was, when did they cook the scheme up? My guess – before I even arrived in town.

It's no fun feeling like a mark, but better to suspect it before-hand (which I haven't always done). Once I'd seen the light, my moves were obvious. I went to bed and grabbed a couple of hours uneasy sleep. Coral was wearing a silk nightgown I liked and she looked pretty fetching. In other circumstances I'd have disturbed her briefly, but the knowledge that a woman is planning to murder you sort of dampens your ardour.

But I was affectionate enough in the morning despite a hang-over. She kidded me about my drinking and I kidded her about putting on weight. MacMurray was having breakfast when I got to the diner. I gave him a haggard look and a brief nod when he raised a questioning eyebrow. He winked, paid his bill and drove off. It was Coral's day to go to Red Springs for shopping. Sometimes she

drove the La Salle, sometimes she got a lift with Pop, who went in
to get sugar for his sourmash or chewing tobacco or something. I
told her the Cadillac had an oil leak which I'd be working on, so she
went with Pop.

As soon as she'd gone I began a thorough search of the house –
cupboards, drawers, boxes, coat pockets, the lot. Coral had kept a
haphazard collection of things over the years – official documents,
letters, photographs – and it wasn't too hard to piece together the
elements of her life story. She was born Coral Anne Smith in Buffalo,
New York, not Denver, although she'd given the date correctly.
From the family snapshots it looked as if she had three brothers and
two sisters, or maybe one of the sisters was her mother, it was hard
to tell. Anyway, a big family, and to judge from the clothes, not
much money. There was a grade school but no high school record.
She'd been married not once but twice, the first time to a Buick
dealer in Chicago. He died in a car crash in 1922. I wondered what
she'd got out of that.

She came west with some money because there were photographs of her in smart clothes in San Francisco and Los Angeles.
In one of the pictures the clothes look a little too smart and the
men a bit too confident. I couldn't be sure, the photo was faded
and cracked, but one of the men looked like my former agent, N.
Robert Silkstein. If it *was* Silkstein's hand on her knee there could
be no doubt that Coral had gone a'whoring. There was no indication
of what had brought her to Three Cedars, but here she was – twice
widowed and a property owner. I'd have laid a bet that an exhuma-
tion and autopsy of Canetti would have showed up something interesting. What's more, she had a lover who talked a ruthless, smooth
line of bullshit and a husband worth twenty thousand dollars dead,
all tied up with a red ribbon.

I didn't hesitate: I packed the clothes she'd bought me into one
of her suitcases, cleaned out all the money in the house (about sixty
bucks as I recall) and stacked the trunk of the La Salle with as much

champagne and liquor as it would hold. I removed every sign of my presence, from razor to nail clippings and a few other things such as the marriage licence and the insurance policy papers, the ownership of which was debatable. I drove the Cadillac across to Pop's and filled the tank and two spare drums which I stowed in the back. The imbecile who looked after the place while Pop was away helped me. By 11 a.m. I was on the road out of Three Cedars. Anyone who wanted to catch me was going to need a better car, of which there weren't many around, and a better motivation for travelling as far and fast as me, which would be pretty hard to find, since mine was to avoid being murdered.

My main thought was to put as many miles between Three Cedars and myself as I could. I didn't go south because that way lay Mexico. After my experiences down there a few years back I had no wish to return.[9] Anyway, I didn't have a passport. I'd just come back from the east and couldn't face the drive again. I went north, intending to skirt Los Angeles and get to San Francisco. From there, the world was waiting. I could go by rail to New York or by boat to Peru or Australia.

I'd had very little sleep the night before, it was hot driving the desert road and I was feeling lousy by mid-afternoon. I stopped in a one-horse town called Rail Spur, on the edge of the desert. The name came from the fact that a branch line from the main railroad had run out to a point near the town when it had been a prosperous cattle-raising centre. The desert had swallowed the grass and the railway line twenty years ago. I got these facts from a tattered pamphlet I found in the hot little room I rented in the adobe brick hotel which was one of the three or four buildings that still held human beings.

I had a nap and took a walk around the place just before sun-down. I have to admit Rail Spur was a pretty place, even as decayed as it was. There was a soft blueness to the light, and the sage brush smelled sweet and clean. The fact that I noticed these things meant that I was starting to relax. There was a general store and a shop that sold Indian curios, both open for only a few hours per day. The board sidewalk had collapsed; the bank was a crumbling ruin and the words 'Post & Telegraph' could just be made out across the front of a building that had been taken over by cactus and stray dogs. I remember thinking that it would've made a great movie location.

Back at the hotel I had a few good belts of New Orleans bourbon before going down for dinner. There were two other people staying in the place, a crazy gold prospector who'd come in from six months in the desert, and an anthropologist who said he was looking for a lost tribe of Indians.

'They're out there,' the prospector said.

We were in the bar, where no one seemed to have heard of the Volsted Act. The anthropologist immediately bought the prospector a shot of rye. I put my empty glass on the bar, and he bought me one too. 'Where?' he said.

The prospector, who must have been over seventy to judge from the absence of hair, teeth and hearing, waved his arm at the desert. 'Out there. Seen 'em.'

The anthropologist leaned towards him. 'Look, Mr . . .'

'Simpson, "Dry Gulch" Simpson to you.'

'Mr Simpson, my name is Keating. I'm doing a PhD at Harvard on these lost tribes. You could be a big help to me.'

Dry Gulch Simpson's washed-out blue eyes went shrewd as he downed his drink. The barman, a thin, consumptive-looking individual, who was also the hotelkeeper, cook and floor sweeper, put a bowl of stale peanuts on the bar. Keating bought us all another drink.

'Mebbe we c'n help each other,' Simpson said.

The barman responded to a burst of Spanish from his Mexican wife in the kichen. 'Food, gents,' he said.

Keating and Simpson didn't reply. The prospector had spread a faded, creased old map on the bar, and they were pouring over it.

'What's to eat?' I asked.

'Tortillas 'n beans,' the barman said. 'Have it here or in the dining room.'

I chose the dining room and sat down with the rest of my whisky and a stein of beer. The room still held ten tables, but there were only four chairs ranged around one of them. The Mexican woman bought the bowls in and I ate alone, washing the hot, spicy food down with the tepid thin beer. Keating and Simpson ate in the bar. I suppose they spilled chilli on the map. The funny thing is, I can still see them, bent over the map, jabbing at it with their fingers and sipping whisky. Maybe they found the gold and the Indians, but I doubt it.

I went to bed early and didn't sleep well. The room was hot and airless, and my stomach was having trouble with the food and the cheap whisky. I should have drunk some water before going to bed and I kept waking up and wanting water but not doing anything about it. If I had got up, things might have been different. I might have noticed something. As it was, I'd finally got into a deep sleep around dawn when the door was thrown open so hard it splintered against the wall. I sat up and looked into the business end of a Colt .44. The man holding it wore a sheriff's uniform and a grin on his big, meaty face.

'Nick Brown?' he said.

'Well, I suppose . . . Yes, I . . .'

'I'm arrestin' you, Brown. The charge is murder.'

CHAPTER SIX

I opened my mouth to speak and he told me to shut up. He took the car keys from the dresser and gestured with the pistol for me to get up. He let me get dressed. Then he marched me out into the early morning chill. The desert didn't look nearly so good now – it was cold and empty and the light was yellow. There were three deputies outside, all armed to the teeth and looking disappointed because I was coming quietly.

'Got 'im, Sheriff Westwood?' one of the deputies said.

The sheriff looked at him. 'No, Eban, he's running across the desert jackass naked. You wanna take a shot at him?'

The deputy looked confused. He certainly wanted to take a shot at something. 'Mean-looking bastard,' he said.

Westwood prodded me in the back with his .44. I gathered he wanted me to move towards the big Dodge with the markings of the county sheriff's office. I did it. Westwood tossed the keys of the La Salle to one of the other deputies who caught them neatly.

'Follow us in, boys,' the sheriff said.

I shivered, not just from the cold. 'In where?'

Westwood looked at me. Now that he was relaxed, the flab hung on his face and body in loose folds. His eyes were small and hard and his teeth were stained yellow by tobacco smoke. He seemed to be considering answering my question, but he decided against it in favour of another dig in the ribs with the Colt. I stumbled across to the Dodge and collapsed into the deep front seat.

The sheriff's driving style didn't suggest a compassionate nature. He rammed the gear shift into place as if he was hammering nails; he thumped his big feet on the clutch and brake and swore at every other vehicle on the road. He drove flat out when he could and when he couldn't. After a few miles I started to sort things out. There were grounds for hope. One, they hadn't shot me and didn't seem to be planning a lynching party. Two, they were bringing in the Cadillac – I could see it raising a dust trail behind the Dodge's dust trail – which meant that I could argue my way out of car theft. The liquor in the trunk might be useful as well. Three, I'd been saved the hotel bill – little victories like that always cheer me up. And, of course, I knew I hadn't killed anybody.

I found a crumpled packet of Camels and a book of matches in my shirt pocket. I offered one to the sheriff who scowled, patted his own pockets, failed to find anything and accepted a smoke and a light. We smoked in silence, apart from Westwood's cursing at other cars and ruts in the road. I thought I'd be lucky to get three questions answered so I'd better make them good ones.

'Tell me, sheriff, who's been murdered?'

He shot me a look that was half hate, half puzzlement. 'That's a new one,' he grunted.

'What is?' I said, wasting a question.

He didn't answer; he'd practically finished the cigarette in four savage drags, and I calculated I wouldn't have his goodwill for much longer.

'Damn it, who's dead?'

He flicked the butt out of the window. 'Your wife, asshole,' he said.

They took me into San Diego which was less than great. Coral was friends with half the cops there. I still couldn't believe she was dead, and they wouldn't tell me anything about it. They fingerprinted and photographed me, gave me a cup of coffee and a sandwich (it was lunchtime by now) and put me in a cell in the basement of the police building. It was a small cell, but I paced it anyway, tramping up and down for an hour or more trying to work out what could have happened. Eventually, I accepted that Coral *was* dead and that I was in trouble. The spouse is always the prime suspect – anyone who's ever been to the movies knows that – plus I'd taken off with the car and what money I could find. I stopped pacing, sat on the hard bunk, smoked and worried.

Westwood came in with another cup of coffee and a female stenographer. The cell was cramped with all three of us in it. He pulled out a sack of Bull Durham and rolled cigarettes for us both. After we'd smoked a minute, he said, 'Let's make this easy on everyone, Brown. Why'd you kill her?'

'I didn't.'

The stenographer had that down in no time. Westwood sighed and finished his smoke. 'Go outside a minute, will you, Nora?'

'I shouldn't, sheriff.'

'But you will, won't you?'

She went out and Westwood shifted his big rump uncomfortably on the bed. 'Look, man. Jus' between us, no one's going to be too upset 'bout Coral. 'Course she was a lovely lady an' all that, but she knew too many things than was healthy for one body to know. D'you see what I mean?'

'No.'

'Goddamn it, Brown. Don't be dumb. Her bein' dead gives some folks clean slates as needs 'em. You plead you was drunk, or crime o' passion or something like that, an' I guarantee you can get out of this with a ten year stretch, maybe less.'

'I didn't kill her. She went into Red Springs to go shopping with Pop. That's the last I saw of her.'

He rolled again, just one cigarette this time. 'She didn't get to Red Springs. She was feeling sick an' Pop stopped a car was heading back to Three Cedars and she got a lift.'

'I'd've been gone by the time she got back.'

'Kid in Pop's store's not so sure about that.'

'He's an idiot.'

'You sticking to this story?'

I nodded.

'You'll fry for it.'

'It's the truth.'

Sheriff Westwood opened the door and beckoned the stenographer back. When she was seated with her pen and pad, he said, 'You refuse to answer any questions?'

'I don't refuse. She went into Red Springs and I left Three Cedars for personal reasons. That's it.'

'You admit you ransacked the house, took the car and the money?'

'I wouldn't say ransacked. The rest, yes. I can explain . . .'

Westwood grinned; it was a terrible sight to see amusement in that fat, corrupt face expressed by a baring of those yellow fangs. Suddenly I broke out in a heavy sweat.

'How're you going to explain the rifle she was shot with having your fingerprints all over it?'

I swallowed hard. I needed a cigarette, a drink, a shave and a bath, and it looked like it might be a long time before I got them. 'I want to talk to a lawyer,' I said.

About two hours and no cigarettes later he walked in. Abe Kurtz was one of the tallest men I ever met. I guess he was about six feet eight, but he looked more because he was thin with it, rail thin. At this distance in time, I can't remember anything much about his face except that it was bony and clever-looking. Likewise I couldn't describe his eyes and hair; you didn't notice such things. He was tall and thin. And smart.

He sat on the bunk and had to tuck his legs up to get them into the cell at all. 'I'm Abe Kurtz. Well, Mr Brown,' he drawled, 'looks like you're in quite a spot. I'm a lawyer by the way. Thinking of representing you, 'less you've got someone else in mind.'

I shook my head. 'I didn't do it.'

'That's interesting. Most husbands do kill their wives . . .' He broke off and laughed softly. 'I mean, when wives get killed. But you say not. Any idea who might've done it?'

'Have you got a cigarette?'

'No, dirty habit. Dulls the brain. I can get some for you though, if you want.'

'Thanks. I don't even know when or where she was killed. The sheriff told me she was shot. That's all I know.'

He filled me in on the details. Coral was found dead in our bedroom a few hours after I'd left Three Cedars. Maria found her; she'd been shot once through the head with the .22 rifle which lay on the floor. There were signs of a struggle and the house was in a mess. The cash drawer was empty. Coral's Cadillac was missing, so was her husband and his clothes and personal effects.

'Problem is,' Kurtz said, 'no one saw her get back to town and as I understand it, the boy at the grain store can't say what time you took off.'

'He's an idiot.'

Kurtz stroked his long, bony nose. 'Now's there's one of your problems, saying things like that. I get the feeling people in Three Cedars don't like you too much.'

'What's that got to do with it?'

'Plenty. It's a strange case. Truth is, here in San Diego, nobody's too mad at you at all. Now you got the facts you need, why don't you tell me all about your strange and suspicious behaviour that got you in this pisspot of trouble.'

I told him. Well, I told him some of it. I kept the Nicholas Brown identity, admitting a few strayings from the truth along the way. When I mentioned the name of Walter MacMurray, Kurtz's nose twitched.

'Insurance man, you say?'

'That's it.' I told him about MacMurray's proposition and how I'd reacted to it.

'I'd say you behaved pretty smart, Nick. You just couldn't anticipate the course of events.'

Something about his cool, logical speech got my brain working clearly. 'That's it! MacMurray killed her. He came by and when he saw that I'd taken off, they had a fight and he killed her. He needed the money. When do we go to court?'

Kurtz took a big watch from his vest pocket and consulted it. He took his time about every least movement.

'In about an hour.'

'Good. I should make a statement. Tell them all about MacMurray and his crooked plan. He's the man they want.'

'Who's going to believe you?'

'What? Why, everyone, it's the truth.'

'It sure doesn't sound like the truth. Sounds like a pack of lies to me.'

I was dashed; the new hope washed away suddenly and I felt, for the first time, like a man in deep, deep trouble.

'What should I do?'

'Anyone ever see you argue with your wife?'

'No, well, Maria perhaps. But nothing . . .'

'Anyone ever see you drunk?'

'Yes.'

'Anyone suspicious that you're not who you say you are?'

'MacMurray had an inkling of it.'

'My bet is he'll offer himself as chief witness against you, along with some of the locals who don't like you. You've got a strange accent, Mr Brown, especially when you're scared. Where *are* you from?'

'Australia.'

'Clean record there?'

Hardly that, I thought. Manslaughter and military desertion at the very least. 'Not quite.'

'Mm. I don't think you'd do too well in court.'

'But I'm innocent!'

'That's as may be. Have you got any money?'

'Fifty dollars.'

'Pity. But let's see, Coral's life was insured for ten thousand dollars, right?'

I nodded.

'If you didn't kill her, you'd collect. That so?'

'I suppose. But, my god, Kurtz, I don't want the money. I just want to get out of this bloody nightmare.'

Kurtz drew his legs up and folded his body forward so that his knees came close to his chin. He levered himself off the bed and stood with his head cocked to one side so it wouldn't touch the cobwebbed ceiling. He stuck out his hand and I shook a fistful of bones and knuckles. 'I'll see you in court for the arraignment, Mr Brown.'

'I thought you said we shouldn't go to court.'

'Have to for now. You say nothing. I'll plead you not guilty. Then you'll have to wait in the gaol for a spell but I'll try to see you're a bit more comfortable than you are here. What brand do you smoke?'

I looked at my nicotine-stained fingers. 'Camels.'

'No problem. Do you like to read?'

I shook my head. 'Well, newspapers, magazines, you know.'

Kurtz smiled. 'I do indeed. I'll see you get some. What sort of work have you done in your time, Nick?'

I shrugged. 'Liquor salesman, soldier, chauffeur, actor.'

'Good,' he said. 'No brains needed for any of them. Just do everything I say and try not to worry.'

CHAPTER SEVEN

I've been before the courts more times than I like to remember. It's worse in foreign countries, where you can't understand what's going on, and you don't know whether you're facing a firing squad or a ten dollar fine. You can usually tell by the degree of the beating you get and the amount of the bribe involved, but not always. As these things go, my arraignment in the San Diego district court wasn't too bad at first. True, they had me handcuffed and the police weren't gentle between the lockup and the court, but I heard one of them say something about 'that son of a bitch, Kurtz' so I guessed I was under his protection.

The courthouse was a whitewashed building with a lot of wood panelling inside. Sheriff Westwood and Eban and a few other county men were there, as well as a couple of officers from the city police. The prosecutor was a ferrety-looking individual in a bow-tie and a suit too tight for him. The judge was an old man whose robes had turned green over time. He was wrinkled like an ancient turtle, and he wore pebble glasses and used a silver trumpet.

'The state charges Nicholas Brown with murder in the first degree,' the prosecutor said in a clipped, no-bullshit-here tone.

The judge's voice was as clear and resonant as that of a man of thirty. 'What's Mr Brown's address?'

Since elocution seemed to be the order of the day, I spoke up, 'Care of the auto camp, Three Cedars.'

Kurtz gave me an angry look.

'Do you appear for Mr Brown, Mr Kurtz?' the judge said. His glasses flashed as he moved his head slightly to take in the whole length of Kurtz.

'I do, your Honour.'

'How do you plead, Mr Brown?'

Kurtz said sharply, 'Not guilty. I'd like to request that bail be set, your Honour.'

The prosecutor was on his feet. A couple of reporters had come into the court and were taking notes. The prosecutor moved slightly to his right so as to be almost speaking directly to them. 'The state opposes bail, Judge. This was a particularly coldblooded killing of a defenceless woman. The community requires protection from violent killers.'

The judge took off his glasses, read something on the desk in front of him and looked up. 'I'm interested in your choice of words, Mr Lewis. I'd like to hear how you'd qualify "cold-blooded" and where you think you might find a non-violent killer. But I don't think your remarks are particularly relevant.'

Westwood was standing at the side of the courtroom, about twenty feet from me and good deal further from the judge. Out of the corner of my eye I saw him moving, adjusting the belt which held his belly in and his gun up. The judge saw him too – God knows what he needed the glasses for.

'Yes, sheriff? You got something to say?'

Westwood cleared his throat. 'Suspect was headin' north, Judge. Clear intention 'o leaving the jurisdiction.'

Lewis nodded gratefully at Westwood. 'The prosecution opposes bail on the grounds that the defendant would be likely to abscond.'

'Mr Kurtz?' the judge said.

Kurtz shrugged. I couldn't believe it – he shrugged! I dug him in the ribs. 'Say something,' I hissed.

'I'm handling it,' he whispered.

PETER CORRIS

The judge smiled, baring a set of white dentures that made him look like a beaver about to attack a pine tree. 'I can see we're in for an interesting trial,' he said. He banged his gavel softly. 'The defendant is remanded to the city penal institution to await trial.'

'All rise,' the clerk said.

I'd been standing the whole time – I felt like falling down and weeping on the floor.

They took me to the gaol which seemed to have as its main function the incarceration of negroes and Mexicans. The guards were white but they didn't welcome me as one of their own kind. The court proceedings had been fairly amiable I'd thought, right up until Kurtz's shrug. I'd fully expected to be walking around free, and here I was, locked up with a few hundred niggers and spics. I had a cold shower, shaved with a blunt razor and was issued with prison denims. Then I was locked in a cell.

A plate of pork and beans and a mug of cold, thin coffee was shoved through a hatch some time later. I ate and drank and pissed into the tin jug provided for the purpose. The hatch opened again and I passed out the plate and cup.

'Pour out de piss, man.'

I saw a coal black hand holding a big enamel bucket. I poured the piss into it. After a few minutes the light went out. I wrapped myself in the thin blanket which was the only bedding, lay down on the hard bunk and went to sleep.

I slept well, but that's a knack I've had ever since my time in the trenches, when I scarcely slept at all. After an experience like that, when you were likely any minute to be blown apart or buried in stinking mud, sleeping in a bed under a roof doesn't present much of a problem, even if the room is a cell. They'd taken my watch along with my fifty bucks and a few other things, like my remaining cigarettes, when I'd booked in, so I didn't know the time when the hatch opened. All I could see was a thin, grey light up at the barred window. I guessed it was about 6 a.m. The cup of coffee that was passed in tasted as if it might have been brewed up from the piss I'd given them the night before. I sipped at it nevertheless, suffered for want of a smoke and wondered what the hell was happening. Kurtz had promised me better conditions.

When the hatch opened again I was desperate for human contact. 'Hey,' I said. 'What's going on here?'

The black hand passed in a bowl filled with something grey and sloppy.

'Gimme d'cup, man.'

'What kind of a place is this?'

'Cup.'

I passed the cup out and he filled it with coffee. I was close to tears. 'Can't you tell me anything?'

'Eat yore grits.'

'Grits?'

I heard him expel a breath that was probably driven part by pity, part by exasperation at my stupidity. That was OK by me – I felt stupid.

'Don' know nothin' does you, man?'

'No.'

'You don' want d'grits, Ah'll give 'em to d' nex' man along. He a real hog.'

I pushed the bowl through the hatch. 'Where am I?'

'Ah'm sorry, boss. You on death row. Dey don' believe in nothin' soft 'round here.'

I sweated in that hellhole for a couple of hours before the door swung open and I was escorted along a cold corridor, up a few flights of steps and into the shower block again, where I was allowed a hot shower, soap, shaving cream and a sharp razor. Then I was taken to a large, clean room where men sat at tables playing cards and reading magazines. Jazz was playing on a radio in the corner of the room, and there was even a vase of flowers.

'What's this?' I asked.

'Remand,' one of the guards said. 'Goddamn playground.'

'Where was I before?'

He grinned. 'Little joke. Solitary.'

I sat in the room leafing through a magazine and wondering what was going to happen next. After a while a guard came across and told me Mr Kurtz was waiting to see me. I went into another room where there was a table and a couple of chairs. Kurtz was sitting down at the table with his feet sticking way out the other side. He waved to me.

'Mornin' Nick.'

'Morning, my arse. D' you know where I spent the night?'

'In solitary. Little joke I fixed up.'

'*You* fixed up. Fuck you. You're fired.'

Kurtz waved for me to sit down. Something in the sharpness of the movement made me do it without question. There was a packet of Camels on the table; I clawed it open and got one lit.

'That's better,' Kurtz said. 'Calm down. I'm handling things.'

'You're doing a great job so far.'

I'm doing fine, and you're going to get out of this if you just shut up and leave everything to me. I've had a talk to MacMurray. He was going to testify against you . . .'

'That lying bastard! I'd like to . . .'

'Now that's what I mean. That's why I didn't push for bail. If you was to go around all fired up like that, you'd spoil everything.'

I smoked and sulked. I remembered how big and fit MacMurray was; I wasn't likely to give him any real trouble. Still, your lawyer's not supposed to keep you in gaol. 'I want out,' I said. 'I'll behave.'

'A few days and you will be out, and with no charges against you. Trust me.'

'I never trust anyone who says that.'

'Wise policy, but in this case you've got no choice. When I've gone they'll put you in with a couple of nice fellows who've done nothing worse than sell a few shares didn't belong to them. You'll get three squares a day, newspapers, radio time. You can play handball.'

'I don't know how.'

'Time you learned. All you have to do is sign this.' He produced a paper from his pocket, unfolded it and handed it to me.

I read the legal language with disbelief. 'This says I owe you ten thousand dollars.'

'Right. You'll be good for it when the insurance company pays off on Coral.'

'Who gets the rest?'

'I'll tell you all about it when it's done. For now, it's better you don't know. So, you've got a choice. Sign this and be out of here by the end of the week, or don't sign it and go back downstairs.'

I signed.

CHAPTER EIGHT

I sat around in the remand section for the next few days, playing cards and reading magazines until my eyes ached, and smoking so much I couldn't tell the difference in taste between bread and meat. The company wasn't very stimulating – a couple of stockbrokers on the run, a bank manager who'd embezzled a fortune and lost it on the horses, a couple of abortionists, a bigamist. I reflected that I might have been guilty of that crime myself, but only briefly. We did some work, mailbag sewing and soap packaging mainly, but time hung heavy.

When the guard said Mr Kurtz wanted to see me in the warden's office, I felt relief flood over me. I finished wrapping the six tablets of soap inside the waxed paper so as not to look too anxious. The guard manhandled me along the way to the administration block, which surprised me. Wasn't I virtually a free man? Kurt was alone in the office. I walked across to the warden's desk, took a handful of cigarettes from the box and handed them to the guard. He looked as if he'd like to use his billy club on me, but Kurtz nodded to him and he stuffed the cigarettes in his blouse pocket and left the room.

'That was dumb,' Kurtz said.

Kurtz was wearing a badly-cut brown suit, a blue shirt with a curling collar, a red tie and lumpy shoes. I supposed he was going into court to defend a farmer when he'd finished here. I sat on the desk and lit one of the warden's Virginias with a gold lighter.

'Why? Haven't you fixed everything? Aren't I on my way out?'

'The murder charge is dropped.'

I left the desk and reached for Kurtz's hand. 'Thank you,' I said, 'from the bottom of my heart. When do I leave?'

'Don't you want to hear how it was done?'

'Sure.'

Kurtz waved me into a chair. He got up and fiddled with a machine on the desk. It was a wire recorder with two big spools and speakers the size of soccer balls. I smoked while he twiddled knobs. Eventually he said, 'Listen to this.' He sat down and stared out of the window. There was a crackle, a hum and then the voices.

KURTZ: I've got it all, Walt – the proposition you made to Brown; a witness who says you were at the auto camp that morning; your tyre tracks; fingerprints on a glass. I can build a case against you at least as good as the one against Brown.

MACMURRAY: You're bluffing.

KURTZ: Call it, then. I'll take what I've got to the sheriff and we'll see how the cards fall. 'Course, I don't want to do that.

MACMURRAY: What *do* you want?

KURTZ: A deal, naturally. That's the American way.

MACMURRAY: Don't talk to me about the American way, jewboy.

KURTZ: You just cut yourself a tougher deal, right there. I'll lay it out for you. You and Coral had picked Brown for a patsy. You got him insured, suckered him into driving around like a maniac and were all set to give him an accident. Brown was going to be barbecued in the Caddy, and Coral'd collect. How'm I doing?

MACMURRAY: You're guessing.

KURTZ: Guessing right. Maybe you had a meeting planned with Coral in Red Springs, maybe some other place, I don't know. But you went by the auto camp and saw the Cadillac was gone. Then Coral arrived and you discovered that Brown had been smarter than you'd thought. Coral called you a chump. You fought. You shot her. I can put you there, don't forget that. You killed a defenceless woman when a crime you planned went sour. That'll get you the gas, Walt.

MACMURRAY: *She* planned it, not me!

KURTZ: Don't flip your lid. There's a way out and it gets you some of the dough, too.

MACMURRAY: Yeah?

KURTZ: That the straight goods about the stiffs you can get from the construction site?

MACMURRAY: So happens it is.

KURTZ: Good. Here's the how of it. You write out a confession saying you killed Coral. You were jealous of Brown. Coral wouldn't leave him for you. Something like that.

MACMURRAY: Are you nuts?

KURTZ: No. Then you put the old plan into action, 'cept the stiff in the burnt wreck is you, not Brown. Get it?

MACMURRAY: Jesus.

KURTZ: If you had the nerve to kill Brown in cold blood, you can do this. You're not killing anybody.

MACMURRAY: I don't know . . .

KURTZ: I've got Brown's marker. He turns over the whole of the insurance payout to me. Your end is two thousand. I was gonnna make it three, but you insulted me.

MACMURRAY: I don't know . . .

KURTZ: Decide, and do it fast.

MACMURRAY: Okay. Okay.

The wire hummed and I yelped, the forgotten cigarette had burned my fingers. I got it into the gorilla's hand ashtray and looked at Kurtz, who would have been smirking if the lines and bones of his face could've permitted it. 'That's outrageous,' I said.

'Now don't go getting all moral on me, Nick. It's a good deal.'

'It's all totally illegal. Did MacMurray know you had that thing going?'

Kurtz ambled across to the desk and switched off the recorder. 'Course not. That's just so you'd know I'm not crossing you.'

'What about the insurance company?'

'Now, that's one of the nicest parts of it. I had a few words to Henry Sexton, who's the claims assessor for American Western and a sort of cousin of mine. He's real happy. They avoid the ten thousand payout they would've had on you, for one thing.'

'That's great,' I said.

'Insurance companies have to pay out sometimes, they know that. This way, American Western gets rid of a rotten apple. Crooked salesman can do a lot of damage in that business.'

I began to feel a little better. I lit another of the warden's cigarettes and puffed.

Kurtz packed the wire recorder into its case. 'Worth talking to, insurance men,' he said. 'Do you know the actuarial facts on cigarette smoking?'

'No, and I don't care to. When do I get out of here?'

'MacMurray co-operated. He wrote the note. Want to see a copy?'

'No.'

'His Packard went off the road last night. Guy was burnt to a crisp. Terrible sight. Doc Parsons identified him, though.'

'That man should be disbarred.'

'Helped to save your hide, Nick.'

I shrugged. 'Can I leave now?'

Kurtz produced a wallet like a small briefcase, extracted a paper and put it on the desk. 'Power of attorney,' he said. 'Sign that and you don't have to be around when the money comes through. Thought that'd be how you'd like it.'

I took a pen from the warden's oak and silver pen set, dipped it in the inkwell and signed. 'You're stalling, Kurtz. What now?'

Kurtz blew on the paper, checked it with his little finger, folded it up and tucked it away. 'There's a problem with the sheriff.'

'Shit.' I slumped down into a chair, remembering Westwood's vindictive, greedy little eyes. 'I knew it all sounded too good to be true. Tell me.'

'He's pissed at missing out on his big arrest. The city police found the note and the Packard and put it together. Had to be that way. Westwood doesn't like it.'

'There's no more money,' I said. 'Eight for you, two for MacMurray. That's the lot!'

Kurtz took a spotted handkerchief from his pocket and blew his nose loudly; a nose that length has considerable resonance. 'There's a solution,' he said. 'It's all logical if you look at it right.'

'Well?'

'The car's the key to it. Westwood wants to prosecute you for grand theft auto. Carries five years, three minimum. State farm, most likely.'

I shook my head. 'I couldn't handle it.'

'Figured that. Now, that car's worth a lot of money, and I understand there's a considerable quantity of quality wine and liquor inside.'

'Take it,' I said. 'For God's sake, take it all.'

There was a discreet knock at the door, and the warden came in. He acted as if he was used to seeing inmates sitting in his office smoking his cigarettes and crooked lawyers packing up wire recorders. He nodded at us, sat down at his desk, lit a cigar and started reading through FBI 'Wanted' flyers – maybe he thought he had some of the poor buggers in there already, and he could claim the rewards.

Kurtz and I went out quietly. The guard who'd brought me there was outside waiting, and Kurtz nodded at him. The guard smiled. 'Well, you're leaving us, Mr Brown.'

'Yes, thank Christ.'

'Don't talk dirty in here, sir, please. Come this way.'

We went down the corridor and through a fenced-off section of the exercise yard, where the blacks and Mexicans were playing

handball and trading insults. A few of them spat at us, and the gobs
of spittle hung on the heavy gauge wire. The guard poked his billy
at the spitters and grinned at them.

'Farm'd be worse than this,' Kurtz said.

'I know.' I had to force myself not to shrink away from the dripping wire.

I was given my clothes and a stall to change back into them. At
the discharge counter, I got my watch and ring back after signing
for them, and was paid six dollars thirty for the work I'd done on the
soap and the mailbags. Kurtz stood by impassively while I endured
these humiliations. I signed the discharge paper.

'Man had some cash on him, I believe,' Kurtz said.

I straightened my shoulders. I've noticed this before and since –
it's a wonderfully confidence-boosting feeling to get out of uniform
and into civilian dress. Some men like the sensation of going the
other way, but not me. 'That's right,' I said, 'fifty dollars.'

The discharge officer looked at me and poked inside a grubby
envelope. He extracted some notes and coins and put them on the
counter. 'Twenty-five dollars,' he said.

I looked at Kurtz, who gave one of his shrugs. The guard cleaned
his fingernails with the keen edge of a tightly folded ten dollar note.

'That's right,' I said, 'twenty-five dollars.'

Kurtz drove me to the Red Springs Greyhound station. He had a
duffle bag in the back of his car which contained some of the stuff
I'd taken from Three Cedars – a few shirts, a change of underwear
and socks, a razor and a few copies of *Readers' Digest*. I got out of the
car, and he handed me the bag.

'Go any place you like from here,' he said. 'But I'd advise you to
catch the first bus, Nick.'

I shouldered the bag. 'Why's that?'

'Sheriff Westwood's given me twenty-four hours.' He checked
his watch. 'Ten gone already.'

It was four o'clock in the afternoon. Several coaches were already lined up in the terminal – I could see their destination boards: Phoenix, El Paso, Bakersfield. I was on my way to the ticket office when Kurt called me back.

'Nick.'

I thought of ignoring him, but then, just possibly, he was going to be useful. I walked back and leaned on the roof of the car. The driver's seat in the Ford had been specially modified to go back far enough to give Kurtz leg room. He looked like a stretched out snake, sitting there.

'What?'

'I told you I'd handle it.'

'You did, Kurtz. You certainly handled most of the money. How about something to get me to New York?'

He grinned and started the motor. 'Got some advice for you, Nick. You're a pretty good-looking fellow, and you look smart and brave, which you aren't, but that doesn't matter. Why don't you try your luck in the movies?'

I turned my back on him and put my hand in my pocket to make sure I still had the thirty-one dollars thirty.

CHAPTER NINE

I can remember that bus depot clearly – it was pretty crowded, with people carrying more baggage and wearing more clothes than they do today. There also seemed to be more small kids around in those days – noisy little buggers, some of them, and others spick and span and quiet. I think kids have changed over the past fifty years but, as I've had very little to do with them, I'm probably no judge. Anyway, I looked along the departure boards and one word took my eye – Butte. I'll never know why – it's not a pretty word or a very interesting one. To this day I still don't know what it means; perhaps it just suited my state of mind at the time – I wasn't much interested in beauty or the meaning of life.

I bought a ticket to Butte on a bus that was leaving in half an hour. Then I went out of the depot, crossed the street and bought cigarettes in a barber store opposite. The barber was a bald man with a thick handlebar moustache. He kept a toothpick in his mouth, shifting its location with his tongue.

'Travelling far, mister?' Flick, flick went the toothpick.

'Butte, Montana.'

'Quite a ways. Be cold up there this time of year. Need a little heart-warmer?' Flick, flick.

This was the secret language of prohibition. I glanced around; no one in the chairs, no one about to come through the door. 'Sure. Pint?'

Flick. 'The best.' His hand went under the counter and came up covered with a towel. I put my duffle on the counter and the transfer was made.

'Two bucks.' Flickety-flick.

I paid him and left the store.

I remember re-crossing the street and going back into the bus depot for a very good reason – I had spotted Sheriff Clint Westwood parked in his Dodge. He watched me, and I had the feeling he knew where I was going, how much money I had and what was in my bag. I guess I scurried into the depot. I got a seat near the front by the window, left-hand side. The bus was only half full, and it pulled out dead on time – 5.20. The watch I had then kept strictly accurate time, not like the crap they sell these days. The seat next to me was empty, and I put my bag on it. I looked the other way as we passed Westwood, and I recall thinking that Red Springs was one of the most boring towns I'd seen, worse than Goulburn, even worse than Yass.[10]

I dozed, then I smoked a cigarette as the last of the light faded. It was early in the evening, and the bus had crossed the border into Arizona, when I pulled the pint of bootleg whisky out my bag. I was very dry and very depressed. It was a flat pint bottle with a long cork that stood up out of the neck so you could get a grip on it. I pulled the cork and took a long swig of the hooch . . . [Browning's voice becomes indistinct at this point, and the recording breaks off. When he resumes he is evidently in the grip of a strong emotion, and it is some time before he regains his customary assured tone. Ed.]

To this day, I'll maintain there was something strange in that bootleg whisky. I say this because I have to admit that the next few years are a blur of separate, unconnected memories, all bad. I don't mean that the pint itself sent me into a tailspin; I'd been under a lot of strain for years and I guess I just cracked. But I've hit the bottle pretty hard at various times since without completely flipping out.

A solid seven-day-bender of the kind old Spence Tracy used to go on is one thing, a lost five years is another. There was something in that bottle, must have been.

Anyway, I was on the skids well and truly. I remember waking up with the horrors in hobo jungles and hospitals; riding freights and being thrown off them; sleeping in doorways, and sometimes in cinemas when I had the price of admission. Through the mists, I recall finding a comfortable spot in a fleapit movie house someplace and staying there for days with a bottle for company. *King Kong* was showing; I missed most of it but saw some scenes twenty times. A monkey on top of the Empire State[11] – and they keep on making it. The movie business is the strangest show on earth.

I don't know where I went or who I met. I must've drunk every kind of alcohol ever invented and probably came up with a few unique combinations. I seem to remember something that tasted of honey and licorice . . . somewhere warm . . . coloured people around . . . somewhere in the south . . . best not to think about it. Prohibition ended in 1933, not that I was aware of it, but I suppose we travelling drunks found life easier. I worked: I was a fruit picker, a bottle washer, a shoeshine man, but never for very long. I worked in a circus cleaning out the animal's cages. I've got scars on my back that a doctor once told me look like healed wounds from a tiger mauling. I don't remember anything about it. One thing I'm sure about – I was never the geek.[12]

It was a woman who pulled me out of it, naturally. Glenda found me in the alley at the the back of the club where she was singing, selling cigarettes, checking hats and doing whatever else she had to do for survival. Christ knows why she bothered, I must have looked like death, but she was a smart woman and she knew men so well that maybe she saw the diamond under the dirt. I woke up one morning on a hard narrow couch that felt like a feather bed after the places I'd been sleeping. There was a clean blanket over me and for a minute I couldn't get used to the smells – of the room, the blanket and myself. I put my hand up to my head and felt a smooth face and cropped hair: where were my shoulder-length rats' tails and beard? I was wearing silk pyjamas and there was nothing crawling in my pubic hair. It was all so strange – the softness, the cleanliness. I moved my hand down and felt myself getting hard.

The voice came from behind me. 'Still works, does it? That's good news.'

I sat up and turned. The movements sent shafts of pain through me, but my eyes came open easily and the breath I drew in was sweet. Before this, getting my eyelids ungummed had been a major operation, and the inside of my mouth tasted like one of the animal cages I'd cleaned. I shook my head, and the pain inside my skull was bearable. 'Who're you?' I said.

The question made more sense than it seems. She was a pale-skinned blonde, about middling tall but thinner than you'd believe. The strange thing is that she had a good shape with it – good shoulders, breasts and hips, but all of it cut on slim lines. She was wearing a white nightdress and her almost white hair hung straight to her shoulders. She had a thin nose and lips – why go on? She was thin everywhere but she had these big, dark eyes that seemed to swallow me up. She was the strangest-looking woman I'd ever seen.

'I'm Glenda Barrow,' she said.

'How did I get here? Where *is* here?'

'I brought you. I found you in the alley outside the club. You're in my apartment.'

'Excuse me, Miss Barrow . . .'

She came closer to the couch; she had a nice walk with a swaying motion that ran the whole length of her body. 'Nice voice you've got. I knew you weren't a bum.'

'I meant, what city am I in, what state?'

She sat down on the couch and put her hand on my leg. 'You're in Butte, Montana.'

CHAPTER TEN

You can take it anyway you like; myself, I prefer to think that I must have subconsciously begun steering my life back onto its true course when Glenda found, or rather fell over, me. Butte, Montana, after all, had been in my mind when I'd last drawn a sober breath and here I was, washed, shaved, clear-headed, and in the very town itself. I've always had a resilience that hasn't been apparent to others. But Glenda, I'd have to say, was one of the people who over-valued me – like my dear old mother and Song Li . . . but I mustn't get ahead of myself.

Glenda described how she'd got me into a car and brought me home. One of the bouncers from the Copper Club, the place where she worked, had helped to get me up to her apartment which was two stories above Meaderville Road. How she got rid of him I don't know, but I can guess. Apparently I was able to move after a fashion – enough for her to wash and shave me, cut my hair, put pyjamas on me and get me to the couch. She was running her hand up and down my leg as she told me all this, and before too long we were reversing the process – undressing and getting good and dirty. I don't know how long it'd been since I'd had a woman and my first effort was pretty hasty. But I recovered fast and we ushered in 1935 in style. (Did I say it was New Year's Eve? Well, it was, and that was probably one of the reasons Glenda took me in. Smart goodtime girls know the rules of the game – she knew that most of the goodtime Charlies would be home with their wives that night.)

We got acquainted quickly over the next few days, as a man and a woman sharing a bed do. Glenda had been born in Chicago. Her parents were Polish, and Barrow was a re-arrangement of some of the letters that made up her unpronounceable name. She was only twenty-six and had drifted west to avoid tough times in the windy city. But tough times followed her, and her job in the Copper Club was only a few steps above the street, and she knew it.

'But what the hell,' she said. 'Better times are coming, ain't they? The newspapers say so.' She was forever reading newspapers and quoting things. The past few years were pretty much a blank to me – I hadn't heard about the Lindbergh kidnapping,[13] for example – but I picked things up fast from Glenda's newspaper snippets, so I didn't seem like a man from outer space. Still, I was caught out sometimes, like the time I showed that I didn't know who the 'Brown Bomber' was.

'Joe Louis, dummy,' Glenda said. 'The nigger heavyweight. I thought you was a sports fan. Where you been?'

'Oh, sure. Louis.' I had to rush out and get a couple of sports magazine to catch up on Camera and Baer.[14] But Glenda was glad to have me around for two reasons: one, we were good together in bed and two, I didn't chew tobacco and spit into the kitchen sink. I changed my underwear and cut my toenails. I didn't wipe my nose on my sleeve. People forget how rough America was in those days. I think I was the first civilised man Glenda ever met.

Glenda was endlessly curious about the wider world but took everything close to home at face value. 'What's your name?' she asked me, straight after our first coupling.

I'd forgotten a lot but not quite that much. Somehow, I wanted to hear it spoken again. 'Dick Browning.'

'Where you from, Dick?'

'Around.'

'You look it. You married?'

'I don't know. I think I might be divorced.'

'Same here. I ain't sure and I don't give a damn. Kids?'

I shook my head. 'You?'

'Nah. I got knocked up in Chi when I was, oh, fifteen maybe. Had it fixed by a butcher, and that was the finish of me as a mother. Can't have 'em. Can't say I mind much.'

My sentiments exactly. In those days, the danger of getting pregnant was always a consideration, and to find a woman with the sure-fire antidote was a great boon. (Women have told me that it's the same these days in respect of vasectomised men. I've often considered putting myself in the category to reap this benefit, but I've never had the nerve.) We got along fine in the little flat all through the long weekend that started the new year. By the evening of the fourth day I was beginning to wonder why Glenda still hadn't got dressed. I wasn't objecting; I could watch her drifting around, all pale and interesting, for more than a few days, but eventually I asked her.

'Butte's a mining town. Miners're the thirstiest workers in the world. Everyone'll be drunk until January third. Club's closed another couple days. I don't drink myself, and you'd be crazy to ever touch it again.'

Right then, I agreed with her. I was tasting food and enjoying coffee and milk the way I hadn't done for years. Glenda didn't smoke, so there were no cigarettes in the flat and no smell of tobacco. I quit smoking without a pang. We listened to the radio and danced in the tiny sitting room. I learned to dance[15] way back from a professional, but I was surprised to find that my five year blackout hadn't robbed me of the skill. I was a little stiff on the turns, but it came back fast. The clean living, the dancing, the eating, the sleep and the sex restored me to good physical condition within a week. Or so I thought.

Glenda went back to work at the club. She took me along and introduced me to the boss, Waldo Fitzgerald. I'd read in one of Glenda's magazines that Butte had filled up with Cornish miners sometime in the nineteenth century. Fitzgerald was the living proof. He was about sixty, big built, with thin, sandy hair and a freckled face that looked as if it had been chipped out of rock.

'Glenda says you're a limey.' He was sitting at his office desk with a cigar going and a brandy by his elbow.

'Not exactly,' I grunted, 'I've spent a fair bit of time over there.'

'Drink?'

This was the first sight I'd had of alcohol and tobacco since I went into the alley behind the club a week back. Some instinct told me his offer was a test. I shook my head and gave him one of the hard-bitten grins I'd been practising in Glenda's bathroom mirror. 'Why don't you say "Job?"'.

'What can you do?'

'Be polite, rude when necessary. Tend bar. Pick a phoney. Use a gun.'

'The politeness, the bar work and the phoney-picking I can maybe use. I got no need for the rest.'

I shrugged. I wanted the drink badly, but I looked at his glass steadily before I let my eyes drift away.

'Know much about this town, Dick?'

'What Glenda's told me.'

He took a sip of brandy. 'Great girl. Heard her sing?'

Another test, I thought. 'In the bath,' I said.

He laughed and almost choked. His colour got very bad. I didn't move and watched him fight for breath. After a minute he was sucking air down again and tobacco smoke with it.

'Most men looking for a job would've jumped up and got the boss some water,' he said.

'I figure the boss should be able to get his own water. If he can't, why's he the boss?'

He laughed again, but high up in his throat this time. He pounded his chest. 'I went down the mine after my old man. Anaconda. You heard of it?'

I nodded. You couldn't spend ten minutes in Butte without hearing of it. The richest copper mine in the world, or it was before the Depression. Glenda had read the latest copper price to me from the paper – five cents a pound. It didn't sound like much.

'Got all sorts of shit in my lungs,' Fitzgerald went on. 'It'll kill me in the end, like it did my father and a couple of uncles and all the other poor buggers as worked there. Well, that's not your grief. I think I like you, Dick. Are you sure you won't have a drink?'

I shook my head, not trusting myself to speak.

'Butte's in the most god-awful slump you ever seen. Copper 'n sheep shit're worth about the same. But I believe things're about to get better. At least for a while. Federal government's spending money on programmes. Most of it'll be wasted of course, stick to the fingers of the desk-jockeys, but it'll be moving around some and I plan to . . .'

'Intercept it,' I said.

Fitzgerald took a dangerously deep pull on his cigar. 'That's it! That's it, exactly. Fly-boy stuff, ain't it? You see that great picture, *Hell's Angels?*'

I shook my head. No one who'd worked on it as I had and seen the broken bodies and the mis-spent money would want to see it.

'You should see it. Great picture! Intercept. Yeah. I'm offering you a job, Dick. Assistant manager. In charge of this 'n that. What d'you say?'

I deliberated for a full minute. I wanted the job although I didn't want the problems that would almost certainly go with it. As I thought, images of the things I'd done over the past five years flitted through my brain like one of the montage sequences you see in the movies. I shuddered. But was Fitzgerald still testing me? I didn't know. I did something very unusual for me – I tried to locate my strongest feeling, apart from the usual one of self-preservation. The words came out automatically, 'I'd have to be in charge of Glenda, among the other things I'd be in charge of.'

Fitzgerald got up and came around the desk. He took my hand and crushed it in a grip that had been built up by using a miner's pick. 'You've got the job, son. Welcome to the Copper Club.'

I took to the job like a lawyer takes to politics. Meaderville wasn't the rip-roistering place it had been in the boom years, but it was still pretty wild, and the Copper Club got a lot of the action. Fortunately, the club attracted a more high-tone crowd than some of the other places. We got mine executives (the ones who'd kept their jobs); members of the families who'd got rich from the mines and stayed rich; politicians and professional men. The occasional mobster from the east taking a holiday until things cooled down showed up. Never any trouble from them. They just wanted to drink, watch the show and go home with one of the girls. I recognised a few of them – including 'Owney' Madden[16] whom I'd known quite well. 'Owney' didn't let on he knew me and I did the same.

The worst customers were the men on the federal payroll – the advisers and consultants and planners. Just as Waldo had predicted, they came through the town spending a lot of the money that was supposed to be pulling America out of the Depression, on liquor and women. I only had to pull a gun once, and that was on a drunken police chief from out of state. Waldo had wised me up to who he was, and it was more the threat I whispered in his ear after the photographer's flashbulb had gone off – catching him with his hand inside the dress of one of the bigger-built showgirls – than the gun that quietened him down.

I got some challenges to my monopoly of Glenda from a few of the hopefuls that worked at the club, but not as many as I would have had before my five years in the gutter. That time had aged me; I had some grey in my hair and I felt stiff first thing in the morning. But, more importantly, I had acquired these furrows in my cheeks and my eyes had sunk into deep, shadowed sockets. Put that together with some scars and a watchful, suspicious attitude, and you had the very picture of a tough guy that not too many were going to mess with. I wasn't really any tougher or braver than before, but I looked it, and that was enough for most of the men sniffing around Glenda.

But Curly Clarke, the bouncer who'd helped Glenda get me home, had seen me in rags with my lips clamped to an empty bottle, and he didn't believe I could hold on to her. Curly was like me in one respect – he could spot a bluffer. I knew it'd happen, and one night he faced me.

'Say, Dick,' Curly said as we were closing up after a quiet night. 'How come you drink ginger ale all 'a time? Pro'bition's over.'

Glenda was behind the bar and I gave her the nod. 'I've drunk everything there is, Curly. I'm just not interested any more. Let's close up, eh?'

'You're lyin'. You'd fall on the floor if'n you took one shot. You'd be lappin' it up from the gutter.'

I gave him the steely grin. 'You're insulting me, Curly. I could take a shot and still whip you with one hand tied. Drop it, let's . . .'

He'd already had a few, and the hand he placed on my chest wasn't all that steady. But the push! It felt like a steam shovel. 'You can't fight,' he sneered. 'You can't do anything.'

I sighed and straightened the set of my tux on my shoulders. 'Don't push your luck, Curly. Waldo wouldn't like me to break any of the furniture over your thick head.'

'You drunk fuck!'

'Shut up, Curly! Glenda's still here.'

'Glenda's a fuckin' whore an' you're a fuckin' pimp, limey faggot . . .'

I took off my jacket and put on my Chicago voice. 'You wanna fight?'

'Yeah.'

'You wanna see me take a shot first?'

'Yeah.'

'Pour 'em, Glenda.'

Glenda poured two shot glasses. I grabbed the one on the left and threw it down. Curly reached for his glass and drank half of the contents in a gulp. Then he removed his jacket. He must have outweighed me by thirty pounds, and not much of it was flab. He had the build of a professional heavyweight gone slightly to seed. I'd watched him in action, and I knew he had the moves. He rolled up his sleeves and went into a crouch.

'I drank my shot,' I said.

Curly reached behind him and picked up his glass. He held it between the thumb and forefinger of his right hand, and he drank it while he flicked out a lightning fast left jab. I just managed to avoid the punch. My countering swing missed by a mile as I intended it to. I circled away with my guard up. Curly brushed aside a table setting as if it was made of papier mâché and so cleared a space about as big as a boxing ring. I was suddenly aware of the wall behind me and the tables to left and right.

'Ready to fight, Dick?'

'Almost.' I avoided his rush and jabbed at him, missing. A flailing right grazed my shoulder and hurt. I considered kicking him in the knee but it wouldn't have produced the right effect. I kept moving back and doing quick turns when I encountered resistance.

'Are we dancin' or fightin'?'

I gritted my teeth and moved closer, hoping to be able to move back quickly enough to take the sting out of his punches. I *had* to land at least one or two, which meant I had to take some. He jabbed. It took me in the eye and nearly tore my head off; somehow I stayed on my feet and managed to avoid the roundhouse right he threw at my ribs. The miss made him grunt and through my one good eye I saw the change come over him. His guard dropped, and I whipped in a quick left that wouldn't have knocked the candles off a birthday cake. Still, it connected with his chin, and he felt it. He swung again but his legs were rooted to the spot and he was off balance. I moved in and hit him hard and very low; his legs buckled, his chin came down, and I met it with my knee which was coming up hard and fast. His head flicked back and his eyes rolled up, white and blank, as he hit the floor.

I won points with Glenda, who'd produced the doped drink on cue, for shrewdness, and I didn't have any more trouble with Curly.

CHAPTER ELEVEN

1935 wasn't a bad year for Butte. The New Deal money was coming in and the copper price was at least holding. There'd been big labour troubles[17] in the town in the recent past, but that all seemed to be over. You wouldn't call it prosperity exactly, but there was money around and it was getting spent. The girls in 'Venus Alley' were doing all right; the right political fixes were in and the town was running more or less smoothly. The Copper Club was doing good business and not too much of the furniture and glassware was getting smashed. Waldo Fitzgerald was happy.

I should've been happy, too, but I wasn't. For one thing, I'd started drinking again and pretty steadily. Butte was always a great drinking town. Billy Sunday had it at the top of his list of sinful places, and I guess he was right. Prohibition barely touched Butte, because the mobsters ran the liquor in over the Canadian border while the cops and politicians held their hands out and looked the other way. I was born to be a drinker and it hasn't killed me yet. I started with a nip or two to keep the cold out, and before long I was up to half a bottle a day and sometimes more.

'You'll go back to the gutter,' Glenda said when she found me pouring a shot just before lunch. (It was a hair-of-the-dog on a very cold morning.)

'No chance, babe. I can handle it.'

'Like you handled Curly.'

I reached out for her. She let me hold her, but she didn't melt into me the way she usually did. 'I can handle it with your help, babe.'

'Not sure I want to help a drunk.'

'I'm not a drunk. Look around you. Is this how a drunk lives?' We'd moved from Glenda's little dump in Meaderville to a house on the south side. I was drawing good money at the club. Glenda's singing had improved, and she was getting a billing and big tips. We were doing fine, but I shouldn't have rubbed it in. It was the whisky talking. 'You were earning it the hard way when I met you.'

'Shut up!'

So we fought and I drank a bit more. We always made it up, and we still had some good times, especially in bed. There was something exciting about Glenda's body that still gets me hot when I think about it. So thin . . . Anyway, I went in for a spot of deception – lacing my coffee through the day and keeping a bottle in the car and generally not being an obvious lush. I was playing handball at a club where the mayor and the political ward bosses and some of the cops hung out, so I didn't develop a gut. The steam baths helped keep me thin, too, plus the fact that I'd started smoking again.

Glenda was a great movie fan, especially musicals, which I more or less detest. But most of the picture houses in those days had double bills, so even if I had to sit through *Top Hat,* I could also see something with Paul Lukas or Brian Donleavy and come out happy. I had to be careful not to let slip that I'd known some of the stars. Glenda went wild over Coop in *Lives of a Bengal Lancer.* I could've told her a few stories about *him*! In the summer we spent a bit of time in the outdoors, swimming at the lake and horse-riding in the woods. With me taking a few relaxing drinks at night, of course.

It sounds pretty good and it was, apart from the sweats and the dreams. I'd wake up in the middle of the night drenched in sweat, from a dream that involved running across no-man's land with machine gun bullets whistling around me, or falling from the top of Doug Fairbanks' model of Nottingham castle. In one dream I was flying a Sopwith Camel and watching one wing fall off and then the other and then going into a spin . . .

'No! No!' I screamed and sat up, shaking and twitching.

'Dick, Dick, it's all right.' Glenda tried to ease me back to the pillow. 'My God, you're drenched. Look at the sheets. I'll have to change them.'

I was hunched in a ball, exhausted and almost asleep again. "S nothing. Doesn't matter.'

'That's the third one this month. They're getting worse, and you're having them more often.'

'Bad dreams,' I mumbled.

'I'm talking about the *sweats.* You've got to see a doctor.'

'Bad dreams. Go 'sleep.'

I thought the dreams were the cause of the trouble, and God knows I'd had enough terrible experiences to dream about. The worst ones involved falling – off horses, trains, buildings – but there were some about hiding in dark, damp places and others about starvation and thirst. All ghastly, but understandable given what I'd been through. I tried to cut down on the drinking a bit and hoped they'd go away. I refused to see a doctor; a doctor is the last person most people see before they die.

One day Glenda came home with a box. I was sitting in the kitchen having a cup of coffee and getting set to listen to the Louis-Sharkey fight on the radio. She started to undo the wrapping paper, and I told her to be quiet because the way Louis was fighting then, if you weren't listening at the first couple of bells you were likely to miss it. Sure enough, it was over in minutes, and I went looking for Glenda. I found her in the bathroom.

'Louis in two,'[18] I said.

'What did he weigh?'

'I don't know, around two hundred I guess. Why?'

'What d'you weigh, Dick?'

I slapped my flat, well, concave belly. 'Me? Always the same. Never varies. Six foot one and a hundred and sixty-eight pounds of sinew and muscle.'

'Step on here.'

'What?'

'I bought some scales. I've tried them and they're accurate. A hundred pounds, that's me. Get on.'

I stepped on the scales and watched the needle flick around the dial. *That can't be right,* I thought.

'A hundred and forty pounds of skin and bone,' Glenda said. 'You're a sick man, Dick. You've got to see a doctor.'

Suddenly, I felt very weak and suspected that a sweat was coming on. I staggered out to the kitchen, lit a cigarette and poured myself a big drink.

Dr 'Spot' Barclay treated Waldo Fitzgerald for blood pressure, kidney stones, gout and a half dozen other things. Fitzgerald swore by him.

'Why's he called "Spot"?' I asked.

'You'll see when you meet him. He's got these liver spots all over his hands. Real ugly. But there's a saying in Cornwall that you can't trust a handsome doctor, and "Spot" bears it out – he's the best.'

I smoked a few cigarettes in the waiting room because I was afraid that the doctor would order me off them. I'd convinced myself that smoking was the cause of my weight loss and sweats. Barclay sniffed my breath first thing. He was only about five foot tall so he just had to leave his nose where it was.

'How much do you smoke, Mr Browning?'

'Ah, well, a pack a day, I guess.'

The doctor went behind his desk and began making notes on a card. I saw the big, ugly spots that covered his hands; they looked as if they were about to jump off the skin and onto the white card.

'Pack and a half that means,' he said. 'Possibly two. Smokers're liars. Universal law.'

I didn't say anything. Well, I could manage without tobacco if I had to.

'Age?'

There was no fudging that anymore, not with the face I had. 'Forty.'

He looked at me and grunted. 'That's honest, at least. OK, Mr Browning, get your clothes off and let's have a look at you.'

I stripped. I had a tan from the swimming and a naturally muscular build so I didn't look too bad – but I had to admit that my bones didn't usually seem so close to the surface. *Probably something to do with the time I spent as a bum,* I thought. *Might need a special diet, maybe.* Dr Barclay poked and prodded me, had me breathe in and out until I was dizzy, bent me over, straightened me up, measured me, weighed me and took spit and urine samples.

'What's that for?' I said.

He sat back behind his desk and made notes on the card.

'What's wrong?'

'Put your clothes on.'

I got dressed and sat in a chair opposite the desk. Automatically, I fumbled in my pocket for my Camels. I got the packet out and shook a cigarette free. I was about to put it in my mouth when I encountered his level, faded blue-eyed stare. 'Don't do that,' he said, 'ever again.'

'Shit!' I crumpled the cigarette in my fingers and threw the mess into his wastepaper bin. 'So I have to quit smoking? What else? A diet?'

'I can tell you a few things about yourself, Mr Browning,' Barclay said, 'and make a few guesses. You've got a naturally strong constitution. Liver's a bit spongy but not too bad considering the amount of drinking you've done. I'd say you had a mild dose of the clap once, but nothing serious.'

'News to me,' I said.

'Right. Well, you're something of a recuperative marvel. At a guess, I'd say your parents lived to a good age. Might even still be alive. Am I right?'

I shrugged. 'Last I heard they were. What's wrong with me?'

'Have you ever done any mining work?'

'Me? Never.'

'Surprising, but I suppose it comes from doctoring in this town so long.'

'I don't understand.'

'I see cases like yours every day, Mr Browning. Probably more of 'em here than anywhere else in the United States.'

'I haven't been here a year,' I yelped.

'Doesn't matter. Classic symptoms – weight loss, high temperature, slight palpitations with high heart rate, hand tremor, cloudy urine. You've got tuberculosis.'

I slid to the floor in a dead faint.

CHAPTER TWELVE

I had to get out of Butte, and quick. I needed a place where I could fill my lungs with clean air a couple of thousand times a day, sleep in the open, drink buckets of clean water and have peace of mind. This was the standard treatment for TB in those days, before the drugs they've got now. Dr Barclay's bans on smoking and drinking were a bit unorthodox, but I was ready to do anything. It was a life or death matter then – the ones who had to stay in the cities and the weaklings who couldn't handle the outdoor life died. But the thought of living in the country filled me with gloom. I couldn't see how I'd have peace of mind out there with the squirrels.

'Maybe I can fix it for you, Dick,' Waldo said. 'And maybe you won't be so down on the New Deal.'

Waldo had come out to visit on the weekend. As everyone knows, Butte is a mile high and a mile deep. The air in the city was pretty much poisoned by the mining operations, but on the outskirts it was clear, if a bit thin. As soon as I'd got the verdict from Barclay I'd moved to a house on the edge of town, to get some rest and think things over. Glenda was talking of us going to Wyoming. Waldo and I were sitting on the porch; I was resisting the temptation to inhale his cigar smoke. 'Fix it so I can go to Wyoming? Thanks.'

'There's nothing in Wyoming but grass. No, I mean fix you up a job here in Montana and not too far away. You could get into town from time to time, and Glenda could come and see you.'

I've never understood the line about not having your cake and eating it, too. Why the hell not? There's plenty of cake. I took a swig of the apple juice Barclay had recommended and asked Waldo to tell me more.

'Ever hear of the Montana State Parks Authority?'

I shook my head. 'No.'

'Not many have. It's got federal money to protect forests and woodlands and such.'

It sounds strange now when everyone's a conservationist or says he is, but it was an entirely new notion then. 'Why?' I said.

Waldo shrugged. 'Don't ask me. All I know is, there's money going into keeping some ranches operating, and protecting the woods and rivers and animals in and around 'em.'

'What about wolves?'

'I don't know, Dick.' Waldo sometimes got impatient with me, I don't know why. 'All I can say is, if you want a job on a ranch, clean air and water and steady pay, I can maybe set it up for you.'

Glenda came out onto the porch, shaking flour from her hands. She'd been cooking Cornish pasties inside. As far as I know, pasties are the only kind of cooking Butte is famous for. I loved them, and Dr Barclay hadn't said anything against them. 'He wants it,' she said. She went across and steadied Waldo's rocking chair and kissed his red, wrinkled forehead. 'Thank you, Waldo. You're an angel.'

A ranch? What we call a station at home, I thought. *All mud and dust and cowshit. Oh, God. There must be some other way.*

But there wasn't and that's how I came to work at the Pratt-Carlisle Ranch on the Tongue River in Rosebud county. Waldo may have been a great fixer, but he couldn't get me any closer to Butte than two hundred and fifty miles with the Rocky Mountains in the way. I went because I didn't want to die. The ranch had been declared a national monument or some such foolishness, and every stone, blade of grass and jack rabbit on it was sacred. It covered about eight hundred acres, some of which was forested land. This meant that the 'tree army'[19] – a bunch of young snot-noses – was involved as well as the Parks Authority for which I worked. The ranch adjoined the Rosebud Indian reservation so the Indian Affairs Department was in on the act. It was close to where the battle of the Little Big Horn had been fought, and that made the area of interest to gawkers, historians and museum types trying to add to their arrowhead collection.

Sometimes it seemed that there were more officials running around the place than stock. I think we carried about a hundred and fifty head of Texas longhorns, and there was a small herd of buffalo, twenty maybe, that were cosseted like sick kids. Those animals were counted twice a month and photographed more than Jean Harlow. There was even a guy came out to study their droppings. I tell you, if a blind, lame camel had wandered onto the ranch it would've been protected.

I had a pretty soft job – riding about reporting on strayed and sick animals and fences that needed mending. I acted as a guide for the busybodies that came around – federal programme men, scientists, journalists, photographers and artists. The ranch house, built in the 1850s, had been modernised, and that's where the staff lived. All men, worse luck. There were five of us; two riders, both 'lungers'; a bookkeeper, who I suspected was there as an alternative to being in gaol; a Swede gardener/cook who couldn't speak English, and a labourer who did what we told him to, when he wasn't drunk.

I got up early, ate a big breakfast and did my rounds, breathing deeply. I shared with George Blair, the other TB sufferer, the task of looking after the five horses and forcing Carey, the labourer, to do his work. At night we played cards with Brian Lucas, the bookkeeper, using a dummy for the fourth and driving him mad by not letting him smoke and only allowing coffee as a throat-wetter. Blair was also under the care of Dr 'Spot' Barclay. The Swede couldn't play cards, the same as he couldn't cook or garden. We got our supplies – groceries, meat and vegetables, no liquor, no tobacco – on a voucher system from the general store in Hardin. The town wouldn't have been far away by car, but was a fairish ride by wagon which was our only means of transportation. Peaceful, restful, you think? Healthy? I would've gone stark, staring mad if it hadn't been for two visits to Butte to see the doctor and Glenda's couple of trips out to the wilderness.

My lungs were the two most important things in the world just then, but I rather resented the way Glenda showed more interest in them than in any other part of my anatomy.

'What's your weight?' she asked, as we were getting set for a quick session on the feather bed. It was November and I'd been at the ranch almost three months.

'Jesus, Glenda, I haven't seen you for three weeks and you want to weigh me like a steak.'

'You still look thin.'

'That does it.' I rolled off and looked at the wooden ceiling beams. We were in the master bedroom of the house. Why I rated it I don't know, but I didn't complain. I let go a little cough and stared at the ceiling.

Glenda knew she'd offended me. 'Ah, honey. I'm sorry.' She began to stroke me. 'Lungers get pretty horny, I hear.'

'That's right. Especially if they're stuck in the bush with men and cattle and buffalo.'

'You do talk funny sometimes, Dick. Stuck in the bush – there ain't no bushes around here. Just trees and grass.'

She continued stroking and before long I'd stopped sulking and we were making the old floorboards of the ranch house jump. After we'd finished, and I'd fought off the longing for a cigarette, we lay back and looked out the window at the clear, pale sky.

'Seriously, Dick,' Glenda said. 'How you feeling?'

'Great. Couldn't you tell?' It was true – I'd put on nearly ten pounds and hadn't had a sweating fit in weeks.

'No blood?'

'Only when I cut myself shaving.'

'Always the joker. So you figure you're gonna mend, huh?'

That sobered me a bit. 'I go for a test in a month. Doc Barclay says that'll tell the story.'

'A month. OK.'

'What's that mean?'

'I'm having a little trouble with Curly.'

'That bastard. Take advantage of a sick man. I'll . . .'

'Don't worry, Waldo's handling it. Gee, that means you'll be coming into town for the test.'

'Right. Let's celebrate.'

'Sure. We can go to a movie and have Waldo over for dinner.'

'A bottle of wine, maybe?'

'No, Dick, and Waldo'll have to do without his stinking cigars.'

'Should be a fun night.'

I put in another month at the ranch. It was cold now but the place was in a valley that trapped some sun and was favoured by a gentle wind that kept everything from icing up. The snow came but it didn't get too deep, and the cattle and other animals sheltered in the hollows and the woods. I went into Butte for the tests.

'Well?' I asked Barclay after he'd examined me. This was a week after he'd taken specimens of everything my body produced.

'Tell you come Easter.'

'Jesus, I'm living from holiday to holiday!'

Barclay stopped his note-making and scratched one of his liver spots. 'You're living,' he said.

I told Glenda one lung was better and one was worse. It didn't make for a good Christmas. I shouldn't have done it, but when the only topic of conversation is your health you've got to have some fun with it. Waldo visited, and he didn't look well. I was grateful to him and I put myself out to be good company. An old Dudleigh Grammar boy can always turn on the charm when he wants to. There was one bright note – my salary was building up quite nicely in the bank in Butte. It was 'everything found' at the ranch, and Carey and Lucas didn't play cards any better than me so we tended to just move a small amount of money around between ourselves. I also had some gold dust and a few small nuggets I'd panned out of the Tongue.

Nothing much happened at the ranch over winter; some animals froze to death, and the Indians killed some. That raised a nice point about 'protected species' but no one was particularly interested. I got on pretty well with the Indians, what little I saw of them. I remembered some of the sign language[20] I'd learned when I'd spent some time with a band in Canada, and we had some fun with that.

I didn't drink and I didn't smoke. I chopped a lot of wood, ate and slept well and felt fine. The papers got to the ranch two weeks late, but it didn't matter because the news was all about how America was on the rise while Europe was going down. I didn't much like the sound of Hitler, although I suppose he had some good ideas about roads and things. I had a feeling I wouldn't get along too well with Stalin either. Churchill'd be more my style – brandy and cigars . . . God, I thought a lot about brandy and cigars.

The thaw was well advanced by Easter. Things were running smoothly at the ranch, but I hardly noticed. I was keen to go into Butte to see the doctor. But a few days before I was due to go Glenda telegraphed the news that Barclay was sick. I've still got the telegram. [A crackling sound on the tape of old, stiff paper being unfolded and a clicking noise, probably Browning putting on his reading glasses. Oddly, Browning's reading voice sounds faintly Australian, unlike his normal speaking voice which is American-accented. The telegram has not been located among Browning's effects. Ed.]

Dear Dick
    The doc isn't too well stop Nothing serious but he isn't working for a couple of weeks stop Guess everything is real

pretty out at the ranch stop I think I could live there forever stop

love stop
Your best girl Glenda

In the end it was May before I got to see the doctor. He brushed
aside my enquiry about his health and got down to examining me.
He made clicking noises as he did so. He hadn't done that before so
I guessed I was either healing well or didn't have long to go.

'Looked at yourself in the mirror lately, Dick?'

'Well, no. Not much call for it out there, and the bathroom's
been bloody cold.'

'You look five years younger than when I first saw you. Filled
out, got all that yellow crap offa your teeth. Eyes're clear. You
don't look like you're ready to cut a man's heart out for twenty-five
cents.'

Well, that was all very good, but the tough look had stood me
in good stead. I wouldn't last long in Butte looking like Ronald
Colman. I buttoned my shirt and tied my tie. I could feel the scrag-
giness had gone from my neck. 'What're you saying, doc?'

Barclay chuckled. 'I'm saying again that you're a recuperating
marvel. You're as good as cured, boy. Another few months on the
ranch and then a clean life and you'll make old bones.'

'That's great! How clean?'

'Real clean. Now get on over and see Glenda. I understand she
and Waldo've got some news for you.'

I shook his hand and made for the door.

'Dick,' he said. 'Stay at the ranch till June, just to be sure.'

I was getting around in a Chevy station wagon I'd hired in
Hardin and driven over the mountains. I drove to the club and went
up to the flat Waldo lived in above the place. He and Glenda were
there, and when I gave them the news Glenda started crying – a
very bad sign.

'Oh, Dick,' she sobbed, 'oh Dick, I'm so happy.'

I gave her a kiss and my handkerchief. 'Sure doesn't sound like it. Hullo, Waldo. Aren't you going to offer me a drink?'

'Dick!' Glenda was suddenly dry-eyed and up on her hind legs. I think that was the moment I knew it wasn't ever going to work out between us.

'Just kidding,' I said.

Waldo's ugly mug was even uglier when he smiled, but he did it so rarely you knew he meant it. 'Wonderful news, son. Didn't I tell you "Spot" Barclay was the best?'

'Hey, hey, don't I deserve some of the credit? Living in the sticks like a bloody monk . . .'

'That ain't quite true,' Glenda said.

Waldo coughed in an embarrassed sort of way and poured coffee for us all. We sat down, me and Glenda on the sofa and Waldo in an armchair. From the way he twitched, I could tell he was busting to light a cigar. It made me uncomfortable – I've never been one to deny people their pleasures.

I drank some coffee and would've traded ten years of my life for a shot of brandy in it. 'Well,' I said, 'what's this news the good doctor says you've got for me?'

'It's more of a proposition, really, ' Waldo said.

Glenda giggled. 'Or a proposal.'

That put me on my guard. I looked at my watch. 'Gosh, is that the time? I have to get the brakes on the Chevy checked before I set off . . .'

'Dick, I haven't got a family, that is, no kids. I've taken a shine to you and I want to put you in my will.'

'That's very handsome of you, Waldo. I . . .'

'Leave you the club, couple houses, fair bit of cash.'

I looked at them both sitting there, smiling, sharing a secret and suddenly wished I was a thousand miles away.

'What's the catch?'

'I wouldn't call it a catch.' Waldo couldn't help himself; he fished out a cigar and unwrapped it. 'There's a condition. I'd like to see you and Glenda married.'

'I'm married already,' I said.

Glenda smiled. 'You *were* married, you told me, and I told you the same. Well, it didn't take but a couple of months for a private detective to find out that I ain't married any more.'

'It's not quite the same thing. I was married in Australia. Different laws, you see. Very complicated . . .'

'So what?' Glenda said. 'You go down to Mexico and get divorced. It's legal here, and that's what counts.'

Waldo lit his cigar. 'Don't like the idea, Dick?'

'You don't love me!'

Like all singers, Glenda could really turn on a good wail when she tried. It wrung Waldo's heart. Not mine. I had to think fast. I stood up and moved towards her, then I stopped and coughed. That always does it – when a lunger coughs, people pay attention. I coughed some more, deeper now and staggered a little. I changed direction unsteadily and leaned against the doorpost, handkerchief out, coughing into it.

Glenda jumped up. 'Dick, what's wrong?'

I held her back with my hand and gasped for breath. 'Have to get back to the ranch. I'll write. Bless you both.'

I yanked the door open and bolted down the stairs. I hit the street running and sprinted several blocks to where I'd parked the car. I was in it and revving the motor before some thought processes started to take hold. I drove to the First National on Silver Street and drew out all but a dollar of my funds. If memory serves, I had about eight hundred dollars. The gold I had at the ranch was maybe worth about that much again. *It won't take you far, Dick,* I thought. *Not in any style, but far enough.*

CHAPTER THIRTEEN

It was a long, hard drive over the mountains back to Hardin, and I was dog-tired when I reached the town. I planned to rest there for the night, drive to the ranch and collect my things and maybe arrange to drop the car at the Billings railhead the next day. At the two-bit hotel the clerk, pasty-faced with slicked-back hair and bad breath, offered me a room at the back over the kitchen.

I put a twenty on the counter. 'Look, I understand your problem. I'm a lunger, right? Blood-spitter. Well, I can tell you Doc Barclay in Butte has given me a clean bill of health.'

The clerk fingered the bill but didn't take it. 'Mister, seein' you've got twenty dollars, I wouldn't care if'n you left a lung in the bathroom. But that's the only free room I got.'

'The Governor visiting?'

'Nope, some movie people. Goin' to shoot a movie out by the Tongue, I hear. All right by me, I hope they stay all summer. You want the room?'

'There's nothing out there but trees and grass.'

'And Injuns. I hear the movie's about Injuns. I hope they pay 'em in cash 'cause no Injun born can hang onto money. Be real good for the town. A dollar for the room.'

I paid and went up the stairs into the narrow, hot, smelly room. I heard sounds of laughter and shouting at various times through the night but I was too tired to pay much attention. I slept late and the hotel was deserted when I went down to the lobby. The clerk's hair was mussed; his hangover was visible in his eyes and on his breath, which smelled worse than before.

'Breakfast?'

He shook his head and regretted it immediately. 'Too late.'

'Where is everybody?'

He reached under the desk for a pint bottle, lifted it slowly and took a swig. It was almost enough to put you off drinking. He swung the register around towards him. 'Now that jus' might interest you, mister. I see you give the Pratt- Carlisle ranch as your address. Well, that's where the movie folk've all gone. 'Bout an hour ago, though how some of 'em could get their heads off the pillows is beyond my understanding.'

'There's no mystery to it,' I said. 'They just don't go to bed in the first place.'

I drove out to the ranch and found the place a madhouse – there were trucks, loads of timber, reels of electric cable and people every-where. Of course, it was all familiar to me from my earlier experiences in Hollywood, but it still gave me a shock. I never expected to see this particular kind of insanity again. I went to the house, planning to get my gold, clothes and a few other things and head off to Billings. I opened the door and there was Lucas, the bookkeeper, standing deep in discussion with a small, dark man I instantly recognised. It was too late to close the door.

'Dick,' Lucas said, 'I want you to meet someone. This is the man I was talking about, Mr Rosson. This is Dick Browning.'

'I don't believe it. By God, it is. "Beverly Hills" Browning!'

We shook hands. 'Hullo, Art. That was a long time ago.'

'It sure was. Say, you look great. This guy's been telling me you . . .'

'I've recovered,' I said. 'Would you excuse us, Brian?' I shep-herded Art Rosson towards the living room. He'd been in Hollywood almost since the beginning. I think he started as a stuntman, then he became a second string director in the silents. I'd met him when

I was working for Fairbanks on *Robin Hood*[21]. We'd talked at a few parties; I couldn't remember any dirt about him and I was pretty sure he didn't have anything on me. He sat down carefully on one of the old chairs and lit a cigarette.

'This is a stroke of luck, Dick.'

Pure Hollywood, you see – start with the good news. The right response is to jab. 'What brings you here, Art?'

'Cigarette?' He extended his silver case and I took one and lit up. I've been smoking ever since. 'Location filming for De Mille. You must've heard about it. We wrote to the Indian Department and . . . God, I don't know, other people.'

I hadn't heard anything, or maybe there were some letters lying around I hadn't bothered to open. I was careless like that; well, I had other things on my mind. 'So what's the movie?'

'It's called *Buffalo Bill.*'

'Christ, we've only got about twenty of the bloody things.'

Rosson threw his cigarette into the fireplace. 'That's a working title. It's about Wild Bill Hickok, Calamity Jane, Custer and the Little Big Horn – everything.'

'Who's in it?'

'Cooper, Jean Arthur, Bickford, Gabby Hayes.'

'De Mille's producing?' I was enjoying the cigarette, drawing deeply on it and sucking it down.

'And directing.'

Hollywood protocol was different then. You didn't say, 'So what the fuck are you doing here?' You didn't say anything.

Rosson cleared his throat. 'I'm the assistant director. We're shooting the Little Big Horn stuff and the Beecher's Island battle here on the Tongue.'

Reluctantly, I tossed the butt into the fireplace. 'Well, it's authentic, I suppose, and that's what De Mille's famous for.'

Rosson laughed. 'Not this time. He's got Hickok in love with Calamity Jane and scouting for Custer and God knows what. Still, it's a big picture. Lots of Indians. Know the Indians around here, Dick?'

I nodded. 'A bit.'

'You ride, don't you? I seem to remember you did.'

'Sure, that's my job here.'

Rosson leaned forward, rubbing his hands. 'Listen. Dick. I got a bad feeling about this. Did you know I worked in Nevada before I got into theatre?'

I shook my head.

'Well, I did – in the goddamn goldmines. It was tough, but it was a hell of a long time ago. I been on Broadway and in Hollywood for twenty-five years. I don't know shit about working out here in the sticks. You do. And you know movies.'

I reached for the cigarette case. 'I've never worked with sound.'

Rosson flicked his lighter for me. 'Have to admit I found it tough myself. Never quite got back to where I was in the silents. Doesn't matter. I need an organiser, unit manager, whatever you like to call it. Sixty a week and you know how it works, Dick. You can make more on the side.'

'How long?'

'Got to be out of here in a month with everything in the can. I've got the crew and all the works. No big-name actors to screw things up. It's all long-shot, bang bang stuff. But it's got to be right.'

'For De Mille?'

'Right. You never worked with him?'

'No.'

'Between you 'n me, he's . . . well, I won't say it. He does great pictures though. I've got to make good on this, Dick. I'm nearly fifty and I need the work.'

I drew smoke into my lungs, held it, and expelled slowly. 'I don't know, Art.'

Rosson looked around the room, taking in the battered rug, the dusty floor and the dried-up bunch of wild flowers in a vase on a window ledge – a legacy of Glenda's last vist. 'You were a guy that liked a little action, as I remember. You getting any action here?'

I shook my head, letting him make the pitch. 'I've been pretty sick.'

'You look fine to me. Tell you what, I can get you work back at Paramount on the main shoot of the picture – some riding and shooting. You've got a good voice, maybe get you a few lines.'

I smoked and said, 'I had some trouble in Hollywood after the Hughes picture. Maybe you heard?'

He shrugged. 'Who hasn't had trouble in Hollywood? That's why the town's got the best lawyers in the country. You need a lawyer?'

'Maybe.' I was thinking it might be time to find out how I stood with my wife and the Australian army, government and police.

Rosson smiled, showing the gold capped front tooth I remembered. 'Get you the best, Dick.'

'I know Cooper,' I said. 'Well, I did.'

'Coop's a good guy. He'd put in a word. Could pick up a nice piece of change, Dick. What d'you say?'

We shook hands, and I was back in the movie business.

CHAPTER FOURTEEN

It took me about two minutes to rediscover the pleasure of having people at my beck and call. Rosson assigned an assistant to me, an eager young Hollywood type, and the first thing I did was have him take the hired car back to Hardin and send a telegram to Waldo and Glenda. The message was something like: 'Recovering from temporary relapse. Overwhelmed by your faith in me. Will see you in Butte next month. Much love, etc.' I figured that would give me all the breathing space I needed.

Then I went to work. De Mille had permission to use the ranch as a base for what would now be called his second unit filming, then it was just called location work. The plans had all been drawn up, and the carpenters built a fort on the banks of the Tongue where the river forked. The fort was supposed to be on an island and where we set up it could be made to look that way. Hollywood. There were Indians to hire, horses to buy and prepare, trees to chop down and cattle to move about. I was able to pad out some of the bills and make a few bucks on the side, just as Rosson had anticipated. We did some filming of the buffalo, but I can't remember whether the shots appeared in the picture or not.

Unusually for the movie business, everything went right. The weather was perfect for one thing, none of the animals or people got sick, and the equipment didn't break down. It was a pretty big operation – several thousand Sioux and Cheyenne, a couple of hundred soldiers from a cavalry unit and the Wyoming National Guard, all riding and strutting about.

Rosson was worried that the Indians and the soldiers might decide to stage the battles for real again to see if the results were the same. In fact, there was a bit of friction between them, but I managed to settle it. I'd been a soldier *and* an Indian (after a fashion), so I was the perfect mediator. After a nasty fight between a drunk half-breed and a still drunker soldier, I got the cavalry major and Medicine Hand, one of the Cheyenne chiefs, together over a bottle of whisky.

'Indians are not allowed to drink whisky,' the major said.

Medicine Hand sank a couple of inches of scotch and stared at him. 'Before the white man came there was no whisky here.'

I poured a slug and drank it before I realised what I was doing. It was my first drink in almost a year. It went down fine and I had another. 'Now that's what I mean,' I said. 'There's an answer for everything. I'm counting on both of you to keep your men in order.'

'My men are disciplined,' the major said. He took a sip of his drink.

'It is a good time of the moon for fighting.'

It wasn't going quite the way I intended. I poured another round. 'Look, we've got an honourable situation here.'

'How?' Medicine Hand said.

The word 'honour' seemed to make the major lift his chin and clench his teeth. Maybe he would've saluted, but he had a half-full glass in his hand.

'We've got two battles to film. The Little Big Horn and Beecher's Island. The Indians win one and the cavalry wins one. What could be fairer than that?'

It was eight o'clock on the night before the first day's shooting. We were all camped out along the west bank of the Tongue. Looking back, it would've made a good scene: the cavalry officer, all spick 'n span but starting to loosen up a bit with the whisky; the old, hatchet-faced Indian chief and me, the tall, bronzed hero, weary from a long day in the saddle, bringing the opponents together. Great stuff. Rosson should've shot it instead of some of the junk De Mille ended up with. Anyway, it worked, and the soldiers and the Indians were happy with one win each and didn't go for a decider. We shot the stoush[22] the Indians won over a couple of days. It was late in May and already hot out on the plains. It was mainly a matter of crowd control – getting the soldiers to bunch up and spread out and fall down in the right way, and persuading the Indians to move into the right places while making the right warlike moves. We had people running around shouting orders while the dust rose and the smoke from the blank rounds drifted over a couple of acres of hill and plain. It looked like chaos on the ground, but the cameras and the editing made sense of it. Rosson was good at placing his cameras, and he must have shot thousands of feet of film. I had a hell of a good time ordering people about, and I even got into the act as one of the Indians. I'd made pals with Medicine Hand, by way of a few bottles of whisky, and he had some of his boys paint me up and fit me out with feathers. I did a lot of whooping and hollering and riding around looking fierce. I didn't try my hand at the bow and arrow stuff – archery from horseback is a specialised skill, and if you don't believe me, try it – but wear a hard hat and plenty of padding.

John Miljan, who played Custer in the movie, wasn't there of course. They filmed his gallant death on the Paramount lot, probably burning old car tyres to create the smoke. It's amazing how much easier filming is without prima donna actors and directors around. De Mille left Rosson alone to get the Little Big Horn footage and, as I say, he did a good job of it. In those days they didn't indulge themselves with re-takes from every possible angle and interminable waiting for the light to be right. The directors knew their jobs – they put the cameras in the right places and made sure there was film in them. You didn't shoot in the rain unless you meant to – there weren't many other rules. I exclude Stroheim from this, of course. He once shot twenty takes of a bare foot that he knew would appear in the movie in a boot. God knows why. It was lucky they never let him loose after sound came in.[23]

With Custer and most of the cavalry and National Guard dead, we turned our attention to the battle of Beecher's Island. In case you haven't seen the movie, this is where the ammunition detail, on its way to supply Custer, is besieged on an island in the middle of a river by the Indians. Naturally, Custer arrives in the nick of time to save them. Again, it was mostly a matter of galloping and shouting and shooting and falling off. The Indians had to charge full pelt into the river, which was tricky, and the shots of the hard-pressed soldiers on the island had to fit in with the stuff De Mille would be shooting on the Paramount lot. But Cecil B. wasn't leaving anything to chance. He had a ten foot scale model of the Beecher's Island fort built and installed in his office at Paramount. He put toy soldiers and Indians in position, and he had a field telephone rigged up so *he* could direct Rosson's direction by remote control.

I'd had enough of riding by this time. Those sharpboned Indian ponies were hell to ride, especially with a blanket and no saddle. The Cheyenne and Sioux had the game pretty well under control anyway, and Rosson got some great shots of them charging into the water, sending up spray and dying in vain. I was occupied mainly in keeping gawkers, who'd drifted in from miles around to watch the filming, out of the way and making sure the river was clear of debris, and that the bottles the Indians and soldiers left lying around weren't winking in the sun. I was pretty busy, but I also found time to do a stint in the fort, potting away with smoky blanks, helping to run the flag up the pole and keeping the bugler's throat (and my own) well oiled with Montana pilsener. So I fought on both sides in the Indian wars, Hollywood version, and had a lot of fun doing it.

But don't imagine I wasn't thinking while I was enjoying myself. I made the most of my scenes as an Indian, wearing a distinctive head-dress and trying to keep well in shot. And I stuck real close to the bugler at the fort who was often picked up by the camera. I knew De Mille liked to get things right, and that meant paying attention to continuity. I was taking out insurance, just in case Rosson thought of reneging on his promise to get me into the shooting back at Paramount.

There was no rain, no whirlwinds, and in those days you didn't get the sorts of holdups you get now, when jets roar across the sky in mid-take, or a helicopter arrives with champagne for the wardrobe mistress. We finished shooting on schedule. Most of the crew left for Billings, but Rosson and a couple of cameramen spent a last night back at the Pratt-Carlisle ranch. We had a bit of a party – that is to say, everyone got drunk. At one point in the evening, Rosson took me aside.

'You did a great job,' he said.

'Thanks, Art.'

'Health all right?'

'Sure.'

He handed me a series of still photos. A couple were of the fort, and various faces and figures were circled in white oil pencil. I was in several shots, half turned away, but recognisable, holding out a canteen to the bugler. 'Nice shots,' I said.

'Yeah, De Mille likes 'em. He wants everyone marked to be on the lot in three days.'

I nodded. 'I'm ready to go.'

'Thought you might be.'

His tone was severe, and I knew what was in his mind; I'd manipulated him, and no one likes that. I grinned at him and shuffled the photographs. 'Look at it this way, Art. You win some and you lose some.' I spread the photos of the Sioux and Cheyenne out on the table. Several faces were circled, but not mine. 'After all, I didn't make it as an Indian.'

Glenda had bought me a set of scales as a present, and I must admit I had a few pangs as I stepped on them in the morning. She'd helped to pull me back from the edge, and I knew I'd always be grateful to her for that. She shouldn't have plotted with Waldo behind my back, but women are like that. I suppose because they haven't got any real power, they have to play things tricky. I said something like this to Jane Fonda once, and she said that if I worked at it I could become a feminist. I've always wondered what she meant by that.

Well, I'd been on the go all day for four weeks, eating like a horse and sleeping like a lamb. I was drinking some, but sweating it out. Stripped to the waist after a wash, I could see that I'd filled out a bit, but I was never one of those chaps to examine himself all over for imperfections. The needle settled on one hundred and sixty-five. I cleared my throat and sucked in a deep breath. My lungs filled easily – no wheezing, no pain. I was clear-headed, apart from a slight hangover, and my hands were steady. I felt fine. I got the gold out from under the bed and packed my few possessions into a small bag. I tried another deep breath – same result. I lit a cigarette (I think that's when I fell into the habit of having one before breakfast), and went through to the kitchen to put on a bit more condition before travelling.

CHAPTER FIFTEEN

We went by first class rail to San Francisco, where Rosson had some business, and I took the chance to cash in my gold. What with that, my salary from the job at the ranch and my earnings for a month on the picture, I had a couple of thousand dollars to take into Hollywood. I stuck like glue to Rosson although I knew my presence was irritating him. That didn't worry me; once we got to Paramount and he'd made the introductions, I'd keep out of his hair – hanging around an assistant director is a sure way to get yourself classified expendable.

We caught a train to Los Angeles, and there was a limousine waiting to take Rosson to the Paramount studios on Marathon Street in Hollywood. I bummed a ride and also one of Rosson's cigars. With money in my pocket, a job to go to and a good Havana in my fist, I was feeling pretty chipper.

'Art,' I said, 'you were going to tell me something about De Mille, but you clammed up. What's he like?'

'Wait and see,' he grunted.

I puffed luxuriously. 'Can't be that bad. I worked for Doug Fairbanks and Howard Hughes. They were both crazy. I've seen a couple of the mad Huns in action. De Mille can't be any worse than them.'

Rosson said nothing.

I was starting to feel a little insecure as we got closer to Hollywood. I'd never worked on a sound film – maybe it'd be harder than it looked. 'I know I'll just be a bit player,' I said, 'and they get treated like shit. But, hell, I have to rate higher than the Indians.'

'Don't be so sure,' Rosson said.

We arrived at the studio. Rosson got me through the gate, and at an office I got a blue pass stamped 'Player'. Rosson gave me a print of the still photo with my face circled; then he pointed to a door, waved and disappeared. I sat around in the foyer of a stuffy building where nothing seemed to be happening. The girl behind the receptionist desk ignored me. I felt foolish and rural in my Montana duds. *Should've bought some clothes in 'Frisco,* I thought. Then Gary Cooper wandered in to ask the girl the time.

'Gary,' I said. 'Hey, Coop.'

He turned slowly and warily to look at me. He'd aged a bit since I'd last seen him in '29, but he still had the same half-asleep look. He scratched his eyebrow. 'Ah . . .?'

I advanced fast, sticking out my hand. 'Dick Browning, don't you remember? I was working on the flying picture with Hughes.[24] We got drunk and I told you about sniping in the war . . .'

'Say, yup. Why hullo there, Dick. Where've you sprung from?'

'Montana, I've . . .'

'Montana, eh?' His eyes seemed to glaze over, making him still sleepier-looking than ever. 'I was raised on a farm in Montana. Prettiest place you ever did see.'

'Is that right? Well, I . . .'

'Good to see you, ah . . .' He turned away. 'What was the time again, honey?'

'Fifteen of two, Mr Cooper,' the girl said.

'That right? Gotta rush.' He smiled at both of us using, I suppose, about fifty per cent of his available candlepower, and ambled away through a door marked Private. The girl looked at me with eyes as wide as the sky.

'Do you know Gary Cooper?'

She was a pretty little thing, dark and well-groomed. *Not a bad place to start in Hollywood,* I thought. I straightened my shoulders before leaning casually across the desk. 'Sure I do. And I'm looking forward to working with him again.'

'My goodness. On what picture?'

'*Buffalo Bill.*'

'What?'

'The picture he's working on now, *Buffalo Bill.*'

That told her all she needed to know. 'Mr Cooper's current picture is *The Plainsman,*' she said. 'Have you got an appointment with someone?'

I showed her my card.

She consulted a pad on her desk. Her voice became thin and hard. '*Plainsman* extras're expected in back lot 3 at two fifteen. If you run, you can make it.'

'I'm not an extra.'

She shrugged. 'Blue pass, extra, what's the difference?'

I quickly found out the difference – not much. Lot 3 was a six-acre paddock which De Mille had converted into the Wild West, complete with Mississippi River, wharf, homesteads, Fort Leavenworth, frontier township, Indian village, hills, valleys and all. I found this out later. For now, I was mustered with a motley herd of hopefuls under a clump of half-grown cottonwood trees that looked as if they'd been uprooted from somewhere and planted there. It was hot and I was sweating inside my suit. I clutched my pass and my photograph and thought, *Why does it always turn out like this for me in Hollywood?*

We waited, and waited. There were about fifty of us, mostly men but with half a dozen women. I tried to keep aloof from the common herd, but I picked up snatches of their conversation:

'I hear it was called *Buffalo Bill* at first.'

'It was called *This Breed of Men* before that.'

'They say Cooper's hung like a buffalo.'

'You hopin' to find out, honey?'

'So, who's he playing – Cody?'

'Nah, Custer.'

'I happen to know he's playing "Wild Bill" Hickok.'

'The hell you say. Who else is in this picture, Geronimo?'

'As a matter of fact, I heard Charlie Stevens[25] is in it. He's Geronimo's grandson.'

'Holy shit!'

De Mille showed up around three. He had a platoon of assistants with him, all looking snooty and reluctant to have to deal with the underlings. De Mille's been photographed more times than the Statue of Liberty, and I guess a hell of a lot has been written about him. They tell me Tony Quinn's got some stuff about him in his autobiography, but he would because he became De Mille's son-in-law. I must look it up one day to see if it's truthful. I know Tony doesn't mention me because someone who read his book told me so. Well, maybe he should have and maybe he shouldn't. I'll leave it to others to judge.

De Mille was as snooty as his offsiders. He looked pretty ridiculous in his high boots with the pants tucked in, loose jacket and flowing tie. The pistol in the polished leather holster was all right on the sets of *The Squaw Man* and *The Plainsman,* but it must have looked pretty strange for *The Ten Commandments.* He wore a floppy hat with a brim which he turned up when he came out of the sun. Occasionally he took the hat off to wipe his forehead and showed a bald skull fringed with dark hair. I had the feeling that he wasn't self-conscious about being bald. Ridiculous he might have looked, but he talked good sense.

'This is a big picture,' he said. 'An American picture.'

That got a fair-sized cheer, in which I joined.

'You all know that making pictures is hard work, and everyone involved earns every dollar they get . . .'

Another cheer.

'. . . including me.'

Cheers again.

'You'll be told what to do, sometimes by me, sometimes by others. Do it, and let's entertain America.'

Then he was off, striding away, and we were left to the tender mercies of the underlings. I tried to push my way through the crowd to the front to catch the eye of a woman with a clipboard who seemed to be writing down names and causing people to smile. Eventually I got close. She wore an eyeshade over a mop of curly hair, and she was all business.

'Say, Miss. Has Art Rosson said anything about me?'

She consulted her clipboard. 'You are?'

'Dick Browning.'

'No.' She turned away.

'Wait!' I brandished the photograph. 'I've got this. I'm in some of the Montana footage. Look. Big scenes.'

She took the photograph and looked at it carefully. 'Mmm,' she said.

I was about to relax when another man produced the same photo. He pointed to my image. 'That's me,' he said.

I looked at him. He was about the same colouring, height and build.

'You're a liar,' I said.

'Miss.' Another photo, another dark six-footer. 'I'm in this picture.'

'You're a liar.' The first interloper and I spoke at the same time.

The woman laughed. 'Boys, boys, give me a break.' She poised a pencil over a sheet of paper and spoke to the second look-alike. 'Name?'

'Brad Smith.'

'Thank you, Brad. Height?'

'Six feet.'

She pointed with the pencil. 'Over there. You're a player. You?' This was to the other man.

'Hunter Thomas,' he drawled in a broad Texan accent, 'an' ah stand six feet tall, ma'am.'

'Thank you. Player. Over there. And you are . . . ?'

'Richard Browning. Six foot one.'

'Too tall. Extra. Over there, please.'

CHAPTER SIXTEEN

That first day on the set of *The Plainsman* was full of indignities and embarrassments I don't care to recall. The extras were treated like cattle, unbranded and headed for the slaughterhouse. I'd had the job of herding extras myself when I was working for Fairbanks, so I knew what to expect. Imagine yourself as a slave chained to an oar in a Roman galley (with a packed lunch and a coffee break) and you'll have some idea of it.

I spent most of the day rolling barrels along the riverboat wharf, and I was sunburnt and bone-weary when I handed in my costume, collected my fin and staggered out the gate onto Marathon Street at 5 p.m. Still, things could've been worse. I was employed on a major movie, which was where fifty per cent of the population of Hollywood would've killed to be; I had two thousand dollars in my satchel and someone to call on. I'd just the strength to flag down a taxi.

N. Robert Silkstein still had his office on Sunset Boulevard, and Miss Dupre was still guarding the fort. Except that it was an even glossier fort than it had been when I'd last seen it, six or seven years ago.[26] The Viking look had given way to a New York, oak-panelled feel, and N. Robert's initials on the door had grown to eight inches high. There was one thing I admired about agents – the hours they worked. N. Robert and his kind had working breakfasts, lunches and dinners. It was a fair bet I'd find him in his office at 6 p.m., unless he was out at a working cocktail party.

Miss Dupre still wore her hair cropped and silvered; she'd put on weight and developed bags under her eyes, but her form was as good as ever. Three people were waiting in the reception area; two of them were asleep. Miss Dupre was a top hand at out-sitting folks. I walked up and sat on the edge of her desk.

'I want to see Bobby,' I said.

'He's got all the hicks he needs.'

'What if I told you I was working for Cecil B. De Mille?'

'I'd say you were a liar. You look like you might be working for the TVA.'

I laughed. 'I've just come down from Montana to do some more work on *The Plainsman*. Paramount.'

'I know it's Paramount,' she flared. 'What're you doing, shoeing horses?'

I took out my pass and the photograph. 'Don't you remember me, honey? Dick Browning? Commander Kelly? *Robin Hood*? *Hell's Angels*?'

She gaped at me. It was the first success I'd had all day. 'Jesus Christ, it *is* you. We thought you was dead.'

'"Were dead", Miss Dupre. Let's watch our grammar, shall we? And I ain't. Buzz him, baby!'

She opened the circuit, and I heard Bobby's voice with all the smooth charm I remembered. 'I said no calls.'

'D'you remember that limey, Aussie, whatever the hell he was? Dick Browning, Kelly. . .shit, you know who I mean.'

'Miss Dupre, get a holda y'self. You still got people out there?'

I leant down and spoke. 'They're all asleep, Bobby, and none of 'em's going to make you any money. This is Dick Browning, and you've got ten percent of me. Remember?'

'I remember the debts your crummy flying outfit left behind. Throw the bum out, Miss Dupre.'

Miss Dupre had recovered fast. 'Mr Silkstein,' she purred, 'Mr Browning's working on *The Plainsman* for Cecil B. De Mille.'

'And he's spoken with Gary Cooper,' I said.

'And he's spoken with Gary Cooper.'

'Show Mr Browning in,' N. Robert said, 'and throw those other bums out.'

I went through the padded door into Silkstein's office not knowing what to expect, apart from greed and cunning. The decor was New York with a touch of London, or what the decorator imagined was London – a silver smoking stand by a club chair drawn up to a fake fireplace and a hunting print on the wall above. Bobby stood behind his desk on what I knew was a slightly raised section of the floor to lift him to above five foot six. He hadn't changed; he was still slight and tight-skinned with an aggressive attitude, like a cruising barracuda. He looked at me warily, something I've got used to over the years. I took a cigarette from the box on his desk and lit it.

'Hi, Bobby.'

He was looking at my clothes, shoes and haircut, trying to estimate my net worth. He didn't like what he saw. 'Said you were working.'

'You owe me, Bobby. I never collected all the money I was due from *Hell's Angels*. You must've picked it up.'

'You left debts.'

'You never settled anyone's debts in your life.'

He sat down and spread his hands in the gesture agents learn at agent school. It means 'Our interests are identical, but mine come first.'

'It was like, seven years ago? We closed all the books on that a long time back, Dick. Let's call it square.'

I squashed out the cigarette in a huge glass ashtray and watched while Silkstein lit a cigar. He tossed the match in the direction of the fireplace and missed by a mile – he was never the sporting type. 'Seven years,' I said. 'Doesn't feel like it.'

'What you been doin'?'

'This and that. Ever hear anything about Bluey?' This was my compatriot and former partner, who'd sold everything out from under me and taken off with my girl.

'Yeah. He flew into a cliff down in Mexico.'

'And Terri?'

He shrugged. 'He was alone. You still carrying a torch for that broad? She cost you plenty. Forget her.'

'Right.' I reached for another cigarette and put the pass and photograph on the desk. Although the documents were only a day old they were by far the most beat up things on that highly polished surface.

Bobby glanced at them. 'So?'

'I need your help.' I explained what had happened. Bobby sat down and took some notes, using a gold pen and writing on a pad that had **SILKSTEIN ENTERPRISES** embossed on the paper. 'The picture's tailor-made for me,' I said. 'I can ride and shoot and all that shit. Rosson promised me a speaking part.'

'You know the rule in this town, Dick – don't hold me to a promise I made yesterday.'

'I want another shot at it, Bobby. I'm past Central Casting and working. Cooper knows me. With a bit of push and shove from you I can get a few lines. I can make it.'

Silkstein drew a line under his notes and put the pen down. 'Can't advance you nothing.'

'I've got a stake. I can see out the year.'

He puffed smoke. 'I dunno. All I ever had from you was trouble.'

'So what's new? Name me a star who isn't trouble.'

'Star? You?'

'I can make it, Bobby. I can ride, shoot, swim, dance, fly aeroplanes . . .'

'How old are you again?'

'Thirty-four, pass for thirty.'

'Mmm, inna medium shot, maybe. They got a good-looking Aussie can do all that, name of Flynn. Ten years younger'n you. Warners 're buildin' him into the new Gable.'

'He's a fake. If he's good looking and he can do all that and act too, he's not an Australian.'

'Did I say he could act? Rin Tin Tin acts better. But he's a star. You musta seen *Captain Blood, Charge of the Light Brigade?*'

'No.'

'Where you been, Dick?'

'Around.' I'd been pretty fired up there for a while but the energy was leaving me. I slumped down in the chair and stared out the window at the sky that was darkening quickly, the way it does in the desert.

Silkstein studied me. Then he spun his chair, reached behind him and flicked open a drinks cupboard. The bottles and glasses were on a kind of lazy susan that revolved slowly. Light from the electric chandelier winked on the glass.

'Drink, Dick?'

Every tissue in my body was crying out for one, but I knew what N. Robert thought of lushes. His father had been one of the greatest of all time. Booze had killed him early, for which Bobby was grateful. But that didn't mean he trusted drinkers. I swallowed and managed to get the words out. 'Never touch it, Bobby.'

Silkstein closed the cupboard. He stood on his little dais again and reached across the desk for my hand. We shook. 'I'll see what I can do for you on the picture, Dick. Mightn't be much, but a start, right?'

'Sure.'

'I gotta few ideas. Leave your address with Miss Dupre out front. We'll be in touch.'

Miss Dupre was still at her desk, and the people were still waiting. She looked at me with a new respect – I must have been with Bobby for half an hour.

'Thought he told you to kick these people out?' I said.

She smiled, baring polished white teeth, too even to be real. 'He doesn't mean it. Can I help you, Mr Browning?'

'You could tell me whether Bobby's got any serious clients at the moment. I get the feeling this is all front.'

She clamped her mouth shut.

'Tell you what, I haven't been in town for quite some time, and I don't know where people are living now. Bobby wants to stay in touch with me, but I haven't got a place just yet. Where would you suggest?'

She took out a card and printed my name on it. Then she looked at me and couldn't resist. 'These days,' she said, 'the people who need a haircut all seem to be living at Venice Beach.'

She was kidding me, of course, but I took a cab down to Venice Beach and found I liked the place. Oil derricks jutted up into the night sky, and the old canals were blocked and overgrown. The roads were narrow, and the walkways were broken down and tended to be clogged by rubbish. I don't know why it appealed to me. I've always like seaside places – perhaps they remind me of home, or holidays, or dirty weekends. I've never objected to oil wells. Who could object to money pumps? Venice Beach had clearly seen better days, like me. Perhaps *that's* why I liked it.

I located a cheap hotel and booked in for a week. A surprising number of the shacks around were for sale and for rent. Looking back, if I'd outlaid the couple of thousand bucks I had then on Venice Beach property I'd be a rich man today. But that's life, as Ned Kelly[27] said. I ate a hamburger as I walked along trying to find the water and get the feel of the place. It *smelled* as if it was close to the sea, but it was hard to get down to the beach through the dead-end streets, overgrown lots and rubbish tips. When I finally located it, the beach didn't impress me. It looked thin and grey; but no Australian is impressed by beaches anywhere else. We've got the best.

The next day was Saturday and there was no work on the film. I didn't get to sleep until around 3 a.m. because that was when the mosquitoes, the bed bugs and the rats went to sleep. When I woke up, scratching at the bites, it was late in the morning, and warm. I washed, shaved and went into the first realty office I came to. I was offered three houses and the agent drove me to them, talking up Venice Beach all the way. The old Victorian ruin on Columbia Drive had the best roof and the least rubbish in the front and back yards.

'Big,' I said.

'That's a plus,' the agent, who said his name was Mr Beer, remarked. 'You can rent out rooms. Have some company and make a few bucks on the side. We can even steer a few people your way.'

Beer was fat and energetic. He wore a yellow shirt, spotted bow-tie and a checked jacket. He skipped up the steps onto the porch and gazed seawards. The rent he was asking was very low and I began to see why. He was looking for a paying boarding house manager. I joined him on the porch and said something disparaging about the paint and the woodwork. We walked around the house, trading criticisms and praise. In fact I liked Venice more by day than by night; I liked the peeling, multi-colour paint jobs, the murals and the seagulls. I was also thinking about my funds. I knew I wanted to stay in Hollywood long enough to have a real shot at breaking into the movies. It might take time and cheap rent would be a big advantage. Then, as now, Los Angeles was deal city.

I drew a dollar sign in the dust on a window and extracted a fifty from my wallet. 'I'll take it, on one condition.'

Beer ate the note up with his eyes. 'Great. Great. What's the condition?'

'You supply me with a car.'

CHAPTER SEVENTEEN

It was a '29 Oldsmobile, one of the worst cars I've ever driven. It didn't want to start and belched black smoke when it did. The gears were mushy, it had no acceleration and the emergency brake didn't work. The others brakes worked too well in the dry and not at all in the wet. Still, it came free and that almost compensated. I insisted on collecting the car as soon as I signed the lease, and also that the Columbia Drive house be cleaned before I moved in. So I spent the weekend at the hotel, or rather in the bars and movie houses of Santa Monica and Century City. I had some catching up to do. I drank some new brands of beer and liquor and I watched movies, particularly the stuff Glenda had never wanted to see – *Saunders of the River, China Seas, Call of the Wild, The Last of the Mohicans*. I saw Errol Flynn in *Captain Blood* and wasn't impressed. For virility, Gable made him look like a virgin sixth former, and I told myself (after a few shots in the bar near the theatre) that I'd tell Flynn this if I ever met him.

On Monday morning I drove the Olds the twenty odd miles to Paramount. Just having a car did me some good. I couldn't take it through the gate, but I got to park it in a space reserved for studio workers. Status is everything in Hollywood. The car won me a small measure of respect at the car park and that won me a fraction more respect inside. Of course, Silkstein had been at work too, and I found myself removed from the extras list and slotted in with the players. It made a big difference – instead of rolling barrels I was riding horses in small cavalry troops; instead of running down the street with my back to the camera I was walking slowly, deep in conversation with the mayor or the stage coach driver.

If you're under sixty you probably haven't seen the picture. Other films from De Mille and Cooper have overshadowed it, but the last time I saw it, about five years ago (admittedly I was drunk and it was on TV at 2.30 am and I fell asleep just before the end), I thought it stood up pretty well. Of course it's a load of rubbish – Hickok and Cody have a falling out; Hickok is bent on stopping the sale of guns to the Indians; Hickok and Calamity Jane fall in and out of love and there's a happy ending.[28] But Cooper was good, and Jean Arthur was terrific. I remember staring at the screen through a haze of Wild Turkey and watching for myself . . . and I remembered . . . [The tape breaks off here while Browning fetches a bottle. He can be heard pouring and swallowing a few quick drinks before his voice resumes, a little slurred but aggressive. Ed.]

Movie star autobiographies are all crap. They make themselves look good and everyone else look bad, or they just make everyone look good. It's not like that in the movies; actors are erratic and directors, writers and producers are crazy. Movie people can go from being sweethearts to vicious bastards in a second. Drink and drugs have got a lot to do with it, of course. It's confusing. Where was I? *The Plainsman,* that's right. Like all movie acting, it was mainly suiting up in buckskins and chaps and waiting around to be told what to do. But I remember a couple of things . . .

There was a scene where an Indian had to deliver a speech about the victory they'd had at the Little Big Horn. Longish speech. The script just had a gap for the words, and one of the script girls asked the players if there was anyone who could speak Cheyenne. I looked around and saw that Charlie Stevens wasn't there. He was playing Indian Charlie in the movie, and since he was Geronimo's grandson I suppose he spoke Apache, if anything, but he still might have been hard to fool. As I say, my time among the Canadian Indians had given me a smattering of their language, and I could string a few sentences together, mainly about rivers and fish and snow and such things, but I didn't think it'd make much difference. Not many Cheyenne went to the movies in those days. I put my hand up and said, 'The moon is waning over the pine trees,' or something to that effect.

'Great,' the script girl said, 'Is that Cheyenne?'

I put on a solemn look and nodded.

'Go to costume and make-up, please. Right now.'

I went to the costume department and got fitted out with a long skirt and moccasins, tomahawk, armbands, braids, headcloth, the works. They didn't have to darken me because the sun had already done that. A few streaks and dabs of warpaint, and I was ready. Then it was off to a fake forest they'd built on the lot – a dozen or so pine trees, boulders and a thicket. There was a clearing with a low burning campfire in the centre of it. As we approached the set, the script girl told me that the Indian had to ride up to the clearing, leading another horse and singing a song. Then he was supposed to get off his horse and approach the campfire. Then Gary Cooper would come out from behind a tree with a gun, and the Indian would spout for a couple of minutes about kicking shit out of the white man.

'Sounds easy,' I said, although my knees were shaking. I'd never spoken a word in front of a camera in my life.

'You can ride, can't you?'

'Sure. I'm a good rider.'

She pointed to where two horses with blankets for saddles and a pack horse were tethered. 'Yours is the one on the left.'

'What's the other one for?'

'It's for,' she looked at her notes, 'someone called Quinn.'

'Eh?'

'Didn't I tell you? You're the stand-in. Mr De Mille's not quite sure about Quinn. If you have to do it, it's better to use another horse. These movie horses don't like having different people up, one after another.'

'Is this Quinn a Cheyenne?'

'Says he is, but he looks more like a Mexican to me. Stand there.'

I watched while Tony Quinn had a conversation with De Mille. One of the technical men looked to be interpreting. They got whatever it was settled, and Quinn used a rock as a mounting stool. *A novice,* I thought. *He'll probably fall off.* He didn't fall. He trotted up all correct, hopped down and stood near the fire, looking around. Then all hell broke loose. I could hear De Mille shouting and Quinn babbling away in Spanish to the technician. *He's blown it,* I thought. *I'm in.* I got a bit closer so De Mille could see me. I understood enough Spanish to gather that Quinn was asking what fucking song were they talking about.

'Get somebody else,' De Mille said. 'Get somebody else.'

I moved forward.

Then Gary Cooper walked up, and De Mille told him to sit down and wait. 'I don't think this kid's going to work out.'

I was about to signal to Coop when he pushed his hat back and scratched his forehead. 'Aw, give the boy a chance. It's his first picture and he's confused. Give him a chance.'

De Mille said something about wasting Cooper's time.

Cooper sat down. 'I don't mind. I saw the kid in the makeup room. Nice kid. Give him a break.'

I could have brained him with a tomahawk. Instead I stepped forward and said a few words in Canadian Indian to Quinn who stared at me. I winked at Cooper who gave one of his slow smiles.

'Hi, Dick,' Cooper drawled, 'what's that you said?'

'I said, "Give the kid a break."'

That got a laugh and suddenly De Mille was all business. 'Okay, we'll try it. Tell him to sing anything he knows in Cheyenne.'

I stepped back and they got to work. Some kind of transformation came over Tony Quinn. He looked taller and older, and when he looked up it seemed that he was directly in touch with the sun and the wind. What he said was pure gibberish, but it sounded great and they did a perfect run-through. I wandered off among the rocks and smoked a cigarette. After a while the script girl came running up. 'Get back there,' she said, 'they're having a fight.'

Hope leapt inside me. 'Who? Cooper and Quinn?'

'No, Quinn and Mr De Mille.'

I hurried back in time to hear Quinn shouting at De Mille about being an Indian, and how an Indian wouldn't ride up and let a white man pull a gun on him. I didn't hear what De Mille said, but there were trees and ropes and about a hundred people standing around, and I expected De Mille to give orders to lynch Quinn. But he didn't. He nodded and waved and the technicians started changing the setup. For a bit player!

They shot the scene quickly. Quinn did his speech, and they got it in one take. De Mille shook his head. I heard him say, 'I hope you'll come back and see me in a few days. I'd like to talk to you about putting you under a personal contract.[29]

[Browning breaks off, and the bottle rattles violently against the edge of a glass. There is a long pause before the voice resumes. Ed.]

It's so goddamned unfair!

CHAPTER EIGHTEEN

Word soon got around on the Paramount lot that Richard 'Dick' Browning Esquire wasn't your run-of-the-mill bit player. I hadn't got the speaking part, of course, but it had been noticed that I knew Cooper and had made a good joke in the presence of C.B. It mattered. I don't mean that I became buddy-buddy with Bing Crosby, Cary Grant and Maurice Chevalier, who were all working at Paramount then, but I was nodded to by certain executives and directors, and I got invited to parties.

I forget what happened at most of the parties for the obvious reason, but I remember the poker games with Paramount players after the day's work was finished. There were some hard-doers working on *The Plainsman* – Lane Chandler, Tex Driscoll, old Franklyn Farnum, James Mason (not the English actor), and Bud Flanagan, who later became a big-time actor as Dennis O'Keefe. Charlie Stevens sat in sometimes. Tony Quinn didn't.

'One Indian in a card game's enough,' Chandler said on one occasion when he was in a fine mood on account of holding good cards.

'If Quinn was here there'd still only be one Indian,' Stevens said.

We all had a laugh at that, although you could never be sure about actors and Indian blood in those days. It was whispered that Tom Mix had a touch, but I don't know whether or not that was true. Certainly you didn't find the Burt Reynolds type, proud of it, around the town. Names were a worry, too. I doubt that Dennis O'Keefe liked to be reminded about Bud Flanagan. William Humphries, who worked on *The Plainsman,* was 'Humphrey' in some pictures and 'Humphreys' in others. We had a Cora Shumway on the picture who was probably stopped right there by her name, and a Stanhope Wheatley who, I guess, sounded too good to be true. God knows what his real name was.

All this is leading to my other main memory of working at Paramount in 1936. After a heavy day's shooting, in which I played a cavalry trooper for one scene and a skulking Indian for another, I sat down for a few hours of poker with some of the other players. Driscoll, the boss of the school,[30] had squared it with the security people for us to use the set of Buffalo Bill's cabin (where the Indians' faces appear at the windows, if you've seen the movie.) We had gas lamps, a pine table and a dirt floor which, I have to say, some of the older players used as a spittoon.

There were seven or eight of us, not a lot of money in the pots and a good atmosphere. (I suppose it was a Friday and we all had money in our pockets.) We'd play a few hands and then drop out to yarn, smoke or go for beer and cigarettes. I was at the table with Flanagan, Stevens and another man I didn't know. For some reason I was wary of him from the start, without any clear reason. I've had these feelings about certain people all my life – probably a head-shrinker could tell me why, but I've never wanted to know. He was a small individual, mid-thirties but smooth-faced, grey-eyed, with slicked-back fair hair and a way of rolling cigarettes that was famil-iar. He dealt.

I looked at my cards. Lousy as usual. Three.'

Stevens sat pat; Flanagan took cards. The dealer took one.

I forget how the bidding went. I know I dropped out early, partly because of my poor hand, and partly because those grey eyes were giving me trouble.

'I'm out,' I said.

The dealer looked at his hand. The grey eyes bored into me across the top of his cards. 'Thass a shame,' he drawled in broad Texan. 'Still, ah admire a man who knows when to quit.'

I grinned and nodded. This kind of hamming was part of the fun.

'Yup, ah do admire that. Ah really do. What's yore name, pardner?'

An alarm bell rang, but too far back and too faintly. I tapped my cards into a neat pile. 'Dick Browning.'

'Is that right, mate?'

The backblocks Australian accent cut through my beer, tobacco and good fellowship fug like tinsnips through lead. I glanced at the other players, desperately trying to gain time. No support.

'And who're you?'

'My name's Colin Carter and I'm from Bourke, New South bloody Wales. You're not trying to tell me you're not Australian are you, mate?'

'I. . . I've lived there.'

Charlie Stevens spat on the floor. 'Are we playing poker, or what?'

'Yeah,' Flanagan said. 'Raise you, Colin.'

'Out.' The grey eyes were like x-rays. He rolled another ciga-rette, and I recognised the style as pure Australian, 1st AIF. *Oh, Christ,* I thought. *He knows!*

'Your buck and my doe,' Stevens said.

I don't know who won the pot. I sat there, trying to place the man sitting opposite. He smoked calmly and kept on looking at me as if I was an interesting painting on a wall. I tried to look uncon-cerned, which is something I'm good at, even when my bowels are turning to water. I struggled to place him but without success. Farnum won the hand, and I was too unnerved to keep playing. I wanted to leave, but I couldn't just walk away from Carter. I left the table, poured a beer from the pitcher and asked one of the other men sitting out what Carter did.

'Stunt man,' he said. 'They say he's good.'

'He looks it.' I watched Carter handle his cards, make quick decisions and shrewd bets. He glanced at me from time to time, and I tried not to look furtive. Stunt men were crazy, dangerous bastards on the whole, best avoided. The only hope you had if one decided to attack you was that he'd be too drunk to be effective. They drank a lot to dull their aches and pains. Carter wasn't drinking. He won a pot and pulled out of the game. He pocketed his winnings and sauntered over towards me. A little guy, five foot six in his shoes, but without an ounce of spare flesh on him. And those damned piercing eyes.

'Ever been to Bourke?' he asked, using the Australian voice.

'No.'

'Great little town, Bourke. Wish I was back there now.'

'Why aren't you?'

He rolled a cigarette in the soldier's way, with both ends twisted and the tobacco loose so it'd burn quickly. You didn't always have time for a leisurely smoke in the trenches. 'I dunno. When the war finished, I sort of drifted around. Got a taste for travelling. Wound up here falling off horses for a living. Were you in the war?'

I nodded. My mouth was too dry to speak.

'What mob?'

'RAF, I was a flyer.'

'Not trying to let on you're a Pom?'

I collected myself and decided to take a firmer line. He was a lot smaller than me after all, and the other men wouldn't have let a fight get out of hand. Besides, a bit player outranked a stuntman. 'Look here, Carter,' I said, 'quit quizzing me, okay? I've spent time in Australia, England, Canada, South Africa and here. Mexico, too. I've been all over. What's it to you?'

He squinted through his cigarette smoke. 'I was in France in June, 1918. We got pinned down by a Hun sniper outside some shitty little town. Bastard picked off two of my best mates. We had a good sniper in the Company, name of Hughes. Only laid eyes on the bloke once or twice, but I saw him shoot a Jerry officer through the head at a thousand yards.'

I remembered the shot. One of my best. I suppressed the impulse to say 'Probably luck' or something just as stupid. I kept my mouth shut.

'We really needed him that day. I reckon he could've got the Hun, or at least made it so hot for him we could go on. I went back to find him, and do you know what?'

I drank some beer.

'Why's your hand trembling, mate?'

'I remember flying over the trenches,' I said. 'Got hit a few times. Well, my kite did.'

Carter ignored that. 'Like I say, I went looking for Hughes, and they told me he'd isolated during the night. It cost us ten good men to get past that bloody sniper.'

'Why are you telling me this?'

'You look like that yellow rat Hughes to me.'

I forced a dry laugh. 'That's ridiculous.' I felt myself relax as I saw the slight doubt in Carter's eyes. If he'd actually been in my unit or had seen me up close and often he might have been sure, even though I'd changed in eighteen years. But he wasn't sure. 'Tell you what, Carter. It's a good story. Why don't you get it down on paper. You might be able to sell it to the movies.'

'Colin,' Farnum called from the table, 'we need a player here with balls.'

Carter gave me one last piercing stare and then went back to the table. I drank some more beer, chatted about the shoot with someone and left soon after. Driving the Olds back to Venice, I sang a few verses of 'Waltzing Matilda' and had a few nips of rye to cheer myself up. What's that quotation about a brave man dying once and a coward dying a thousand times? Never seemed quite right to me – the coward *survives* a thousand times.

I kept a weather eye out for Carter and was careful not to get caught on my own in some isolated part of the lot – remember, they had small deserts and ravines and forests and all sorts of miniature bush-whacking places. I didn't see him more than once or twice and, although he looked at me as if he'd like to hang me from a tree branch, he didn't make any trouble. The filming went on quickly and smoothly. De Mille knew what he wanted, and how to get it. I did all I could to get myself into prominent positions, but there were plenty of others doing the same thing, so it wasn't easy.

One day I was standing around waiting for a take when Cooper wandered over to me. He was carrying a Winchester rifle and a book. He put the book down on a log and sat on top of it.

'Guess you're not going to read that, Coop,' I said. 'Less'n you can read it with your ring.'

Cooper laughed. 'I haven't read four books in my whole life and I don't plan to start now. People're always giving me books to read, telling me what great movies they'd make. You read much, Dick?'

I shook my head. 'When I'm reading, I always feel there's something else I should be doing.'

'Right.' He raised the Winchester. 'Now, hunting's a different matter. Remember how you told me you was a shooter in the war?'

I did remember. It was in a night club when I was working on *Hells Angels*.[31] 'Sure,' I said.

'You told me something about sighting, but I forget quite what it was.'

I took the rifle and automatically lifted it into the sniping position, which is a particular shooting style – very loose but compact, making the smallest possible target. Open sights and a lot of shoulder support.

'You sure look the part,' Coop said.

One of De Mille's assistants was signalling for Cooper, and I handed the rifle back. Then a feeling as cold as a wind from the Canadian Rockies crept over me. I glanced to my left and saw that Colin Carter had been watching us from no more than twenty feet away. My mind raced. What he'd seen was bad enough, but if Carter spoke to Gary I was a dead duck. But stunt men didn't just amble up and chat to major stars, and Cooper wasn't very approachable by nature. There was only a couple of days' shooting left, and then God alone knew where any of us would be. If I could just keep out of Carter's way for those few days, I reckoned I'd be all right. He could spread rumours about me, of course, but in Hollywood any talk about you, even if it's bad, is better than no talk at all.

Nothing happened the next day. On the last day of shooting they were doing the scene in which Jean Arthur takes a bullwhip to one of the town roughs. I suppose they kept the scene until last in case she broke her arm using the whip – she was a small, frail-looking woman, but she made a lot of movies and is still alive, so I guess she must have been pretty tough. I landed the job of the rough, and I was glad to get it. I got suited up in flannel shirt and dungarees and fitted out with a holster and a six gun. Then I went to the set – dirt road, horse trough, hitching rail, store fronts with nothing behind them, boardwalk.

They were setting up the scene, and for the first time in Hollywood I was given a chair to sit on. Jean Arthur was sitting a short distance away. She lifted the bullwhip and waved to me. I waved back.

'Hey,' I said to one of the technicians, 'can she use that thing?'
'She's had lessons from an expert.'

It was an early afternoon in August, and pretty hot. I was sweating from the heat, even though my chair was in the shade, and nervousness. I wanted to make a good impression. Dick Harlan, the assistant director, was putting the finishing touches on the set-up; De Mille was on his way.

'We'll run it through,' Harlan said. 'Take your places.'

I walked out into the sun and stepped to the left and to the right as we mimed the mêlée that preceded the whip-wielding. Jean Arthur, in buckskin shirt and denims, did her part to perfection so that she and I ended up facing each other – me with my gun out and her with the whip uncoiled.

'Okay,' Harlan said. 'Looks good. Let's run through the whip scene.'

I watched, horrified, as Jean Arthur moved away and handed the whip to Colin Carter. He lifted it like an extension of his arm and cracked it over his head. The sound was like a shot, and I felt it go through my guts.

'We'll fake it,' Harlan said. 'Colin, show Jean how close she needs to get.'

Carter nodded and coiled the whip. I stood rooted to the spot, too frightened to run. I had an empty gun in my hand, and a hundred people were watching me. Out of the corner of my eye I saw Cecil B. De Mille approaching down the street. Carter's arm moved in a motion like a striking snake; I heard the leather whistle in the air, and then my right arm was on fire from the shoulder to the wrist. I screamed, dropped the gun and collapsed into the dust. The pain was intense, and I remember thinking, just before I fainted: *I must be the last man to be flogged for deserting the Australian army.*

CHAPTER NINETEEN

That was the end of my work on *The Plainsman*. They carted me off to the infirmary and treated my arm, which remained blue-black for a couple of weeks. I carried it in a sling and got a bit of mileage out of playing the hero wounded in the line of duty. I got a few days extra pay as compensation, too. I don't know what happened to Colin Carter; with any luck, he broke his neck the next time he fell off a horse.

Silkstein was happy. 'You done great, kid,' he said. 'Just great.'

'I didn't get a credit or a contract.' I winced as I moved my arm.

It was a week after the flogging, and we were in his office; he got a cigarette out of his gold-embossed box, put it in my mouth and lit it for me. 'Takes time. You got noticed, that's the big thing. I can get you work.'

'Bit parts, no doubt. I thought you had something more ambitious in mind.'

'I do. I do. I'm working on it. Look, take a couple of weeks off. Relax, but stay in shape. There's a boxing picture coming up could be right for you.'

'Oh.'

'You don't like boxing? Thought you said you done some ring work back in Australia?'

'Yes, sure. Boxing's fine. I can handle myself.'

Silkstein patted my shoulder, and I winced again. 'Sorry, kid. Don't worry, we're on our way.'

He was sounding like a boxing manager already. I asked him how his enquiries into my situation vis-à-vis the Australian authorities was going, and he said he was working on it. That was N. Robert. He always said he was working on it, but I never actually saw him work on anything.

The arm was healed enough for me to drive as long as I took it carefully. Making sure no one was around to see me, I slipped the sling off, started the Olds and drove back to Venice. I was feeling fairly positive; I had money in the bank, the prospect of more work and an interesting place to live. I didn't like the sound of a boxing picture too much. Boxing was something I'd always tried to avoid at Dudleigh, usually by faking some injury or illness. I was always big for my age, so when I actually had to get in the ring, I usually had a reach and weight advantage that kept me out of trouble. I took some nasty ones on the nose though.

The house on Columbia Drive was called 'Casablanca',[32] which you mightn't believe but it's the truth. Cleaned up, with the porch boards nailed down and the guttering fixed, it didn't look so bad, and Mr Beer had had no trouble finding tenants. Getting them to stay and pay their rent was another matter. I had the big front room with the balcony that looked south-east. You could see the water if you hung on and bent yourself to look back down the side of the house. It wasn't something to do when you were drunk. There were five other rooms, four of them a good size and one not much bigger than a cupboard. The rents were on a sliding scale according to the quality of the rooms. I forget the prices, all I know is, I lived rent-free and had a little pocket money left over when the rooms were full. When they weren't, I had to cough up.

'Job works on an incentive system,' Mr Beer said. 'You keep the place nice, people stay, and you're in clover.'

'You've got too kind a view of human nature.'

'Me?'

I did my best to get the plumbing fixed and the rubbish carted away and to provide roach killer and mouse traps, but times were still hard and people were on the move. Especially in Los Angeles, where many are called but few are chosen. I had a couple of rules – no women, a month in advance, no cooking in the rooms, no obvious blacks. By the last rule I mean that I let rooms to light-skinned negros who could pass as white, or to smooth-talkers who said they were from Kalamazoo or some such place. If they didn't look like field hand niggers or behave like animals, it was okay by me, as long as they could pay the month up front.

It made Casablanca an interesting place to be, all this passing and various humanity. There were actors, of course; some on the way up and some on the way down; James Murray stayed a few weeks when he was really on the skids. Some musicians, mostly drunks and misfits, who played their instruments at all hours, hocked them for the rent and flitted. Cornell Woolrich was at the house for a few weeks, until I threw him out for bringing back sailors in the early hours of the morning. A guy who said his name was Jim Thompson stayed for a month or so. I heard him typing and shouting and drinking in his room. Then he got a big cheque and left. He might have been the guy who wrote the paperbacks,[33] I don't know for sure.

But there was a more settled population, like Eben Cartwright, the schoolteacher, and Renee Duluth, the magazine illustrator and the boxer, Larry Spielberg. The schoolteacher was trying to be a writer, Duluth was painting in his spare time and Spielberg was fighting smokers and working days in a fish cannery. I never learned anything about writing or painting, but Spielberg and I used to spar and fool around a bit, and I picked up a few boxing tricks I figured would be useful if Silkstein got me into a fight picture.

We had some great parties that summer – Casablanca was a good partying house, with its big rooms and easy access from the kitchen to the outside The parties started in the afternoon and went on through the night into the next day. Movie people came along; not the snotty ones earning the big money, but the bit players and technicians and others whose names, at that time, didn't mean anything to anyone. They mean something now: David Niven came once or twice, but he was so high on *kif,* which was what they called marijuana then, that he didn't recall a thing about it. I used to try to convince him in later years that he'd been to the notorious Casablanca parties. As I recall, his usual response, sweetly said of course, was something like, 'Shut up, you colonial oaf, and see if you can organise me another gin.'

John Farrow, who later became famous as a writer, director and father, turned up at Columbia Drive a few times. He was an Australian, and I think he came out of homesickness. I spent as little time with him as I could, as with all Australians in Hollywood, of whom there were a good number. They tended to ask uncomfortable questions about your parents and what you did in the war and how you got your work permit. I usually managed to pass myself off as British or South African. Once I even made out I was a New Zealander, which mystified everybody.

I've got a photograph somewhere taken at one of these bashes – maybe thirty people lolling about on the balcony and striking poses on the scruffy grass in the backyard. All smoking, and not necessarily tobacco – reefer-smoking wasn't a gaoling matter then. I tried it a few times myself, but I never really cared for it. I remember wandering into a movie house when I was high on *kif* and sitting through a few sessions of *Mutiny on the Bounty.* I came away very frightened of the sea and ships. Had nightmares about drowning for months afterwards.

Alcohol was the popular party drug, of course. You can see some of the bottles and jugs of muscatel. All the men are in open-necked white shirts, and with wide-legged trousers pulled up under our armpits – ghastly. The women who came along weren't the type to weigh themselves down with gloves and hats, and they looked pretty in their summer dresses and ankle-strapped shoes. Especially Belinda Douglas.

I fell heavily for Belinda. She was one of the most beautiful women I'd ever seen – medium-tall, dark with huge eyes and chunky white teeth that she only had to show briefly to get my blood pumping. She came to a Casablanca party with someone who left early. She found me on the balcony, smoking a cigarette and feeling a little blue. I'd had no word from Silkstein about the next picture. I felt a hand go into my pocket and take out my cigarette case. I turned quickly, and there she was – black hair and eyes lit up in the match flare. And those teeth.

'Thanks.' She handed back the cigarette case. 'You the host?'

I nodded.

'Actor?'

'Trying to be. Richard Browning, how do you do. What's your name?'

'Belinda Douglas. Let's go to bed.'

Not many minutes later she was saying, 'You're out of practice, Dicky. Wait a bit while I finish up.'

She masturbated quickly and effectively, while I lay rigid beside her. When she'd finished she snuggled up. 'That was nice.'

'Glad you liked it,' I said.

'Quit being huffy. You really put me in the mood, lover. I'm sure we'll have lots of fun together.'

She had a deep, throaty voice that oozed sex, and she never used words like 'don't', 'not' and 'can't'. It was exciting to be around so much positive thinking. We were both in the mood again within a very short time, and I played my part much better.

'Told you so. Now, where are we? I was a bit squiffy.'

'My bedroom.'

'Any women's clothes around?'

'What the hell d'you mean?'

She laughed. 'Hey, hey, don't worry. You did fine. If you're queer you're a great actor, and who the hell cares anyway? No, I mean like things your wife or girlfriends might've left.'

'I'm out of practice with women, as you indicated.'

She punched me lightly, well, not so very lightly, on the mouth. 'Listen, Dicky. I like you. I like big, dark, handsome men who've been around. I like to drink with them and screw with them. Come to think of it, small fair men're OK, too. But I like you, and I think we can get along.'

She showed the teeth at the end of that speech and I was ready to die for her. 'But. . . ?' I said.

'Don't sulk, don't complain, laugh, be nice. Know why?'

I shook my head, but not sulkily.

'I'll tell you. They're going to blow up the world in ten years' time.'

It was all I could do to stop jumping out of bed. If there's one specimen of humanity I cannot stand, it's the religious crazy. I eased away a bit, I'm sure. 'Who's they?'

'The Krauts, the British or us, what difference does it make? You ever heard of nuclear fission?'

'No,' I said truthfully. That was the first time I'd ever heard the words.

'It's physics. I like to read about physics. It's this way, split the atom and you get enough energy to blow the fuckin' world apart.'

'Why would anyone want to do that?'

'You could make bombs that'd do it.' She clapped her hands. 'Goodbye London, goodbye New York, goodbye Berlin.'

'Jesus. But can that be done, splitting the . . . whatever it is?'

'Atom. They're working on it, brother, they're working on it. And if they get it right the party's over, so let's have a good time.'

I grabbed her and kissed her hard. I wanted to feel the teeth press against my mouth. If she wanted to have a good time because mad scientists were planning to blow up the world, that was all right by me. She returned the kiss and we made love again. It had been a fair while for me, and I was stoked up. Belinda was impressed.

'Nice going. Now, about the clothes. Any women live here?'

I shook my head. I was ready for some sleep.

She got out of bed. 'Shit. I'll be leaving dressed the way I came, and I don't like that. On the other hand,' she leaned down and kissed me, 'I sure did come.'

'Leaving? I don't understand.'

'Belinda doesn't stay overnight, honey, and she tries to change clothes every twelve hours. I mean *really* change clothes. I'd steal your pants and a sweater if you weren't so big. You going to drive me home to Culver City?'

I'd have driven her to Nome, Alaska. I scrambled out of bed, dressed and drove her to Culver City. On the drive she told me a little about herself – born in Alamogordo, New Mexico, on 16 July, 1910. She had a Mexican grandmother.

'She and my mother died on the same day, and I left.'

'Accident?'

'No, my father shot them.'

And that was all she ever said about family life. She'd been around the movies since she was seventeen, getting regular work in Westerns as a Mexican dish, or in costume pictures as a slave girl. She made a living and didn't care enough about the business to try to move up a slot.

I was crazy about her, but I was crazy about making it in the movies too, which was just as well, because Belinda wasn't a one-man woman. I got as much of her time as she allowed me, but I did get her to stay overnight once – that was after we celebrated the news that Silkstein had got me into *Kid Galahad* with Robinson and Bogart.

CHAPTER TWENTY

I was excited when I saw the script. I knew I was too old to play the bellhop fighter managed by Robinson, but there was a good part for the tough champ managed by Bogart. I figured the more scenes I got with Bogart the better.

'I've been picking up tips from Larry Spielberg,' I told Silkstein.

'Larry what?'

'He's a fighter.' I mimed a few punches. 'I know the moves. Well, I always did, but fighting styles change and now . . .'

Silkstein lifted his hand so that his pinkie ring glinted in the light. 'Yeah, yeah, that's great, Dick. Just don't get your hopes up too high.'

'What d'you mean? It's a great part.'

'What is?'

'Bogart's fighter.'

'You ain't Bogart's fighter, kid. That part's for Bill Haade.'

'What am I, then?'

Silkstein shrugged. 'Who knows? Whatever they ask you to do – sparring partner, stumblebum, whatever.'

I sat down in one of Silkstein's leather armchairs. 'I won't do it.'

'You got anything else?'

I shook my head.

He knew he had me and could afford to be magnanimous. 'This is a Warners' picture. It'll pack 'em in. Do it right and you'll be noticed. Trust me.'

'You said . . .'

'I know what I said, and I'll deliver. Keep on with Spielberg. Stay in shape. You'll hear from me. And, Dick, I hear you've got that faggot writer staying at your place.'

'Woolrich? I threw him out.'

'That's OK. You've been seeing Belinda Douglas?'

There was no keeping anything from Silkstein. I nodded. 'Anything wrong with that?'

'Not a thing. Has to do you good. You get her to sleep over?'

I answered without thinking. 'Last night. We . . .'

'Great. When you're on your way, we'll put that around.'

'You'll do what!'

'Just kidding, just kidding. See you, Dick. Keep your nose clean.'

When I told Belinda the news, she got angry. 'That Silkstein's a bum. You ought to be with Myron Selznick.'

'Sure,' I said nastily, 'like you are.'

Belinda laughed. 'No agent for me. There's no chance I'm going to pay a guy ten percent of what I make and suck his cock too.'

Belinda had a way of speaking that won her a lot of arguments.

We were eating lunch in Schwab's drugstore on Sunset Boulevard. Belinda was wearing a black and white suit that looked expensive but was a bit crumpled. She saw me eyeing the crushed collar. 'I was over at some place in Malibu last night. Everyone running around buck naked. I smuggled this out in a towel. Nice, huh?'

'You'll get caught one day.'

She shrugged. 'I always leave something behind. Fair exchange's no robbery. Seriously, lover, if you want to get ahead in this business, you've got to start making some moves.'

She bit through a celery stalk (as well as being the first person to talk about nuclear fission, Belinda was the first vegetarian I ever met); as usual, the sight of her teeth did me good. I smiled and made a rude gesture with a breadstick. 'Such as?'

'When's the shoot start?'

'September sixteenth.'

'Good. I start in *Show Boat* the same day.'

'What're you doing in it?'

'Showing my little brown tits down on the levee, what else? Point is, we can throw a party at Casablanca. Who's directing your punch picture?'

'Michael Curtiz.'

'Invite him. And Bogart and Robinson and everyone else.'

'They won't come.'

'I'll invite some of the right girls. They'll come, or some of 'em will. I know a young one Flynn's interested in. Maybe he'll come.'

'I keep hearing about Flynn.'

'He's a dish.'

'Have you . . . ?'

'Nope. Look, you've got to get Curtiz or Bogart or even some of the technical people at Warners to take some notice of you. That way you can make this picture work for you.'

'Do I invite Silkstein?'

'Fuck Silkstein.'

'Have you?'

'His father. Once. Damn near squashed me to death.' Belinda fished a small diary out of her jacket pocket and thumbed through it. 'How about September fourteenth?'

'Fine,' I said.

She scribbled in the diary, then she giggled. 'I wonder what the girls'll be wearing.'

Organising a party in Hollywood in those days was mostly a matter of making a lot of phone calls and ordering up a lot of booze. You had to be careful not to invite people too recently divorced from each other, or the lovers of wives and husbands who didn't know their partners *had* lovers. In the sweller parts of town you needed a couple of kids to park the cars, and waiters and a barman. In Venice you parked youself and drank out of the jug if you had to. It was a good idea to have a word with the cops. A few dollars in the right hand ensured that they'd cruise by keeping an eye out for car thieves and sitting on anyone who complained about the noise.

'Who'll be there?' the police sergeant asked me, after I'd contributed to his welfare fund.

'Bogart, I hope.'

'I mean broads, Mac. Are all you actors queer?'

I gave him one of my manly grins. 'Maybe you'd like to come down to Sammy's gym and spar a few rounds with Larry Spielberg and me?'

Spielberg had recently won a six-rounder at the Figueroa Auditorium – decked a tough Mex in the second, and the sergeant knew it. 'No offence, Mac.'

'None taken, sarge. Jean Harlow's invited. Maybe Betty Grable'll come along and bring her legs with her.'

'Maybe I'll drop by for a glass of water.'

There was nothing formal about a Casablanca party. You asked people, and they came or they didn't, drunk or sober. Bogart wasn't a big star then, so you could count on a message left at the Warners front desk reaching him. Robinson was bigger and you couldn't be sure. I had no idea what women were being asked – that was Belinda's department. I was pretty sure she wouldn't bother about Garbo.

There was only me and Spielberg in residence then. It being September and school holiday time, Eben Cartwright had gone to the south, Mississippi or Georgia, to visit his folks and Duluth was serving three weeks in gaol for drunk and disorderly. Spielberg invited some guys from the cannery and the gym.

'The boys from the gym'll keep the guys from the cannery in order,' he said.

'Great,' I said, 'we've got the makings of a real party here.'

I wasn't short of money, and the booze and food were an investment, so I spent up big. I got in ten cases of beer, three of champagne, plenty of hard liquor and jugs of muscatel and dago red for the rough element. Belinda made a rum-based fruity punch she called a 'W. C. Fields special'. The beer and wine went on ice in the kitchen and bathroom. We had hams and bread, olives and cheese, a couple of pounds of crackers and nuts and six different kinds of salads. We scattered packets of Camels and Luckies around the place and I hired a phonograph and a stack of records, mostly jazz – drinking, dancing and sex music. It was a nice, warm day that promised a soft night. On those nights, if you stood at one of the upstairs windows and listened real hard, you could hear the sea.

Belinda, Spielberg and I spent all day on the arrangements, and we really worked. I tidied up the yard while Belinda washed up a couple of weeks of dishes. Spielberg swept the house out and stowed the empties and the old newspapers and magazines under the house. I didn't see another soul, didn't turn on the radio or take my usual walk to get a paper for the sports results. We were fairly bushed by the evening so we took a few quick drinks to get ourselves going. I remember thinking that everything seemed very quiet, but that's often the way it is before a party. I danced with Belinda, and she danced with Spielberg. We ate a bit to stop from getting too stewed. A few of the cannery and gym men turned up and started to demolish the food and beer. By 10 p.m. I was getting worried. A good party never kicked off before 11, but this was ridiculous. *Someone* should've arrived, even if it was only the gate-crashers or the lushes who swiped all the bottles they could and left early.

At 11.30 I said, 'No one's coming.' A beer bottle hit the cement out in the yard and shattered. 'I mean, no one from the movies.'

Spielberg had been trying to keep pace with his buddies, and he was almost paralytic. 'Too bad,' he muttered. 'You think I can win the title, Dick?'

'I don't understand.' Belinda was dancing slowly in the middle of the room by herself, nursing a drink and crooning softly. She wore a little black dress that she could get out of in about three seconds, and I knew that was exactly what she was planning to do.

Just before midnight, the telephone rang. I lurched over and picked it up. A cannery worker dropped one of the records just as I did so and I had to stick a finger in my ear to close out the crash and the noise of his cursing. 'Hullo, hullo. Who's this?'

'It's Robert Silkstein, Dick. Sorry to call so late and under the circumstances, but I finally got it worked out, and I hadda tell you.'

'What are you talking about?'

'My idea, to promote you.'

'No, no. What circumstances?'

'Ain't you heard?'

'Heard what, for Christ's sake?'

'About Thalberg. He died today. The whole town's in mourning.'

CHAPTER TWENTY-ONE

I must have hung up on Silkstein. I don't remember doing so the way I don't remember anything much about the next twenty-four hours. We held our own wake for the boy genius Thalberg, dead of pneumonia at 37, and I bet there was no one in Los Angeles drunker than me and Belinda Douglas, Larry Spielberg and the guys from Sammy's gym and the cannery. We drank a devastating amount of everything on offer, ate a lot of the food, smoked all the cigarettes and smashed a lot of the records. The party that never was put a big hole in my bank account and all for nothing. I was still hung over when I arrived at Warners on the 16th to report for work on *Kid Galahad.*

The first person in the picture I saw was Bogart. He squashed a cigarette out on the edge of the ring they'd mounted as a set. 'You look worse than I feel,' he said.

'Impossible.'

'British, eh? I didn't think there were any limeys in this picture.'

All those 's' sounds got me a little bit wet. 'I'm not British.'

'So long's as you're not a Kraut. Too many Krauts in this business.'

I don't know how Billy Wilder, Marlene Dietrich, Paul Muni, Fred Zinnemann and Fred Astaire[34] would have felt about that, but Bogart never did care much about how people felt about him. I worked hard in the film; I was KO'd several times by different boxers, I skipped rope in the gyms, did roadwork and got in and out of cars. I spoke only two words. I said, 'Thanks, boss,' to Bogart, and they cut it out of the final print.

The picture took rather longer to shoot than expected, because of an accident to one of the actors. It was the usual Hollywood schemozzle. The actor they got to play the champ, Bill Haade, was a big guy who'd been a steelworker. He came to Warners with a reputation of being the all-Navy heavyweight boxing champion. Fact was, he'd never had a pair of boxing gloves on in his life. First boxing scene he's in, he gets knocked flat on his face by Wayne Morris. This is no good – he's supposed to fall on his back. He didn't get up either, and they found that he'd twisted his ankle in falling. They shot around him but he was on crutches for a couple of weeks and getting paid for doing nothing. I heard he bought real estate with the windfall and got rich. The luck of some people.

Warners were notorious for their small budgets and, apart from Haade's bonanza, there was no fat in *Kid Galahad* – no freebies, as they'd say today. Curtiz was a good, economical director (for some reason I've always admired the directors that didn't waste money – maybe I should have gone into production instead of acting). He knew what he wanted, and how to get it quickly.

Kid Galahad was a good picture, and I came out of it with some money and fitter than I'd been in years. I could run five miles without puffing, skip for an hour, and I could even move around in the ring to make it look as if I knew how to fight. In fact, I knew how to avoid getting hurt and not much more, but for movie work that was enough. I don't know how many takes have been spoilt in movies by actors not getting out of the way of a punch quickly enough. Never happened to me.

It didn't do much for my career though. Ironically, Belinda's role in *Show Boat* turned out to be bigger than she expected. I went over to her apartment in Culver City during the shoot and found her all dressed up like a Mexican fan dancer. She threw a knife at me as I walked in, but I could see it was one of the rubber prop knives and I caught it.

'What's this?'

'I'm rehearsing my next role.'

Bit players didn't usually have a 'next bit', let alone a 'next role'. I poured myself a drink and watched her stamp her feet and hammer the castanets. She wasn't bad. She finished with a swirl of skirts and a flash of the teeth that made me put down the drink and reach for her.

'Later,' she said. It was the closest I'd ever heard her get to saying no. She went on dancing, and I went on drinking, and when we finally got into the cot I was lousy. She compensated herself the way she had the first time.

'Selznick saw the rushes,' she said.

'David?'

'No, Myron.'

I put on my Bogart accent – I fancy I was one of the first people to do that. 'Too many goddamned brothers in this business.'

Belinda didn't laugh. 'He's taken me on. He's getting me into a picture where I play a Mexican dancer. I get to talk, sing and kill a man with a knife – it sounds like fun.'

'It sounds like money, too. How'd this happen?'

'I guess it must've been the teeth. There's a shot of me smiling in the rushes.'

'Well, I hope they won't get in the way.

That got me a laugh and a vicious dig in the ribs. 'It's not like that with Selznick. It's all business. But since you mention it, let's see if we can't do a little better this time.'

We did better.

But I was jealous and envious and frustrated. I took it out on Larry Spielberg in the gym, or tried to, but he was so much better than me he just tied me up in the corners, tapped me once or twice and danced away. Like all good fighters, he had the knack of turning

an opponent's aggression back onto him. That's how it looks anyway, and that's how it felt. A few days after my talk with Belinda,
I was sparring with Larry, whaling away to the body and cursing
under my breath. He propped me with a stiff right; I started to
black out and he held me up, carried me to the corner stool.

'Hey, Dick. You OK? I didn't mean to hurt you, but you were
acting kinda crazy there.'

He shoved the smelling salts under my nose and my brain
cleared. 'I *am* crazy. Feel like getting drunk?'

'Hell, no. I gotta fight in a week. Whatsa matter? C'n I help?
Cause you'n me's pals, Dick. I mean, you let me run for weeks on my
rent when I was broke an' I don't forget things like that.'

He didn't know I was afraid to ask him for it on account of the
muscles and the fists, but it never hurts to have people think well
of you. I let go one of my brave, I'm-just-one-hell-of-a-guy grins,
and we went off to shower. Under the spray, I got to thinking about
Casablanca, and how much longer I could stand the place. I could
afford an apartment in a better district, and it might do my movie
rating some good. Truth was though, I found the place interesting.
When you don't read or play the violin or write poetry, you need
something to occupy your mind. That is, unless you're a gambler or
such a lush that emptying bottles is a full-time occupation. I liked
cards and horse-playing and the numbers and lotteries and drinking, but I seem always to have had time left over to study people.
Not that it's done me any good, but that's not the point.

Just then at Casablanca the residents were myself, Spielberg,
Duluth (in between gaol terms), Eben Cartwright and a cousin of
his he'd brought back from the south. There was no physical resem-
blance. Cartwright was tall and lanky with a lock of dark hair falling
across his forehead; the cousin was a scrawny yellow-haired hayseed
with buck teeth and one shoulder higher than the other. He wore a
suit jacket too big for him, over a checked shirt and old army trousers hitched up high. On his feet were boots, what else?

'Mr Browning,' Cartwright said in his formal way, 'I'd like you t' meet m' cousin.'

'How do,' the cousin said.

'Fine.' I shook a hand as hard as a horseshoe. The callouses were so rough and sharp, it hurt to touch them.

'This's Abell Buzzacott, Mr Browning, an' I was wonderin' if it'd be all right for him to rent the small room a while. I c'n pay.'

'Sure.' The small room had been vacant for weeks, and every paying customer was a load off my back. Abel looked at Eben every time someone spoke, as if he didn't understand English. 'Will you explain the rules to him, Eben? He . . . ah, looks as if he hasn't spent a lot of time in the big city.'

'Abel's a little slow, I admit. Fact is, down home people call him A.B. which is his initials right enough, but they also mean he hasn't mastered the alphabet too well. But he's a good god-fearin' man with the right principles.'

To me, Abel's principles looked like deep holes for fence posts and tight bales for hay, but I was curious about Cartwright, who seemed like a mixture of scholar and something else I couldn't quite place. 'What principles are those, Eben?'

Cartwright handed his carpet bag to his cousin and pointed to the stairs. Abel ambled off, now carrying two fully stuffed bags as if they contained nothing heavier than candy floss. 'I'd like to talk to you about that some time, Mr Browning.'

'Happy to,' I said. 'Perhaps you'd like to let me have Abel's rent in advance in accordance with the rules of the house.'

Cartwright counted out the money, adding in the tariff for his own room. That put me in a good mood. 'We had a little party while you were away, and you'll find a bottle or two left over if you look around. Feel free to drink up whatever you fancy.'

Eben turned with one foot on the bottom stair. 'I don't drink, sir. Neither does my cousin. That's one of the principles I mentioned.'

I nodded and lit a cigarette. When in the presence of saints there's only one thing to do – sin all you can. I went on with my life – squiring Belinda around, keeping an eye on things at Casablanca, waiting for N. Robert Silkstein to call and tell me he'd landed a big one. I didn't hear from him for some time after the phone call on the day Thalberg died. I decided I must have offended him and that I should make amends, but I never seemed to get around to doing it. In the end, it was him who contacted me. I answered the phone late one night after driving Belinda home. Silkstein always phoned late, to give you the feeling that he was working for you, twenty-four hours a day. The phone was on the wall in the hallway; we all used it and put nickels and dimes in a jar to pay the bill. I noticed that the jar was full – someone had been making a lot of calls.

'Howsa kid?' Silkstein said. 'In shape?'

'I'm OK. Look, Robert, I'm sorry about hanging up on you. I was . . .'

'Forget about it. You was having a party the day Thalberg croaked. You didn't invite me, incidentally, but forget about that too. You got talked about for your lousy timing.'

'Can we forget about that?'

'Sure, sure. Remember I said I hadda sure-fire idea to build you up? Get the attention you need?'

'Yes. Have you got a part for me? What is it?'

'Not a part exactly. There was a coupla things looked good for you, but they didn't work out.'

'The story of my life.'

'Don't go getting negative on me, as the editor said to the chorus girl. Haw, haw.'

I laughed dutifully. I *needed* N. Robert. An actor in Hollywood without an agent immediately sank back to being an extra and was at the mercy of Central Casting – which basically meant you chose between humiliation and hunger. So I laughed.

'Here's the thing. First, this has gotta be a secret between you 'n me. You don't breathe a word to anyone, understand? Not Belinda Douglas, not your confessor.'

'I'm not a Catholic, Robert.' Eben Cartwright walked past just then and nodded in a friendly way.

'Just a manner of speaking. I hear you been sparring with a real fighter?'

'That's right. Larry Spielberg.'

'I'll have to try to catch him. I like a good fight, once in a while. I also hear you did all right punch-wise in the picture.'

'I did most of my acting on my back. And no jokes, Robert. Ah . . . it's late. Can I call you tomorrow?'

'No, you gotta hear it now because this is Day One, whatever the hell time it is.'

I yawned. 'Going on for 3 a.m., Bobby.'

'I'll give it to you short and sweet. I got it all set up. I've been laying the groundwork. This is the greatest stunt since Johnny Weismuller went over Niagara Falls in a barrel.'[35]

'Short and sweet, Robert.'

'You're gonna fight Errol Flynn. And you're gonna knock the sonofabitch out.'

'What? You must be crazy. Flynn's ten years younger than me, and he'd outweigh me by ten pounds at least.'

'The guy's a cream puff. You can tell by looking at him, and all those broads he runs around with must be weakening him. Stands to reason. And he drinks like Prohibition's coming back tomorrow. I been checking up on him.'

'What else have you been doing?'

'Spreading the word that you say he's not a real Ossie. And that he can't fight. 'Course that's not strictly true. I understand he did a bit of fighting in Australia.'

'Jesus, Bobby, you don't know what you're saying. The fight game in Australia's the toughest in the world. If he fought there, he can fight.'

'You scared of him?'

'No, but. . .'

'You can take him. And one thing, Dick. Don't mess up that pretty face of his. Warners wouldn't like it.'

CHAPTER TWENTY-TWO

'What's this I hear about you and Errol Flynn?' Belinda said.

'God, not you too! How far has this thing spread?'

We were in a bar on Hollywood Boulevard. Belinda was about finished with *Show Boat* – she was wearing what looked like a riverboat whore's costume, all plumes and flounces – and she was feeling skittish.

'It's all over town that you've called Flynn a fairy. I suppose that's why you keep looking over your shoulder? In case he comes in.'

I kept my head very straight. 'I am not looking over my shoulder. The whole idea's a mad scheme of Silkstein's.'

Belinda sipped her martini. 'Do you some good if it works. Flynn's not the most popular guy in town.'

'I have no intention of brawling with Errol Flynn. It wouldn't be dignified.'

Belinda put her big white teeth into the flesh of the olive in a way that made my palms sweat. 'I know you can box,' she said, 'but I gather Flynn's no slouch. You hear what happened when they were making *Light Brigade*?'

I closed my eyes. 'Tell me.'

'Seems they were somewhere in the San Fernando Valley doing a horse scene. Flynn was playing an officer whether the cameras were rolling or not, and one of the extras decided to take him down a peg or two. He stuck his lance up the ass of Flynn's horse and the critter bucked Flynn off into the dirt. A couple of hundred people thought it was very funny.'

'What did Flynn do?'

'Pulled the guy off his horse – big bastard apparently, stunt rider or something, and they went at it. Took a while, but Flynn knocked the shit out of him.'[36]

'Thanks, Belinda,' I said, 'that was just what I needed to hear. Think we should go? How about your place?'

I'm staying. Hey, look, there's Errol!'

I whipped around, and Belinda laughed herself silly.

It went on like that for a few weeks. I skulked around Hollywood when I had to go near the place, jumping at shadows. Mostly, I tried to stay in Venice and have Belinda come to me. I tried to conceal this from everybody, of course. I swaggered when I thought I was safe and made disparaging remarks about *Don't Bet on Blondes,* one of Flynn's first Hollywood films, which was so bad it isn't even shown on late night TV. I also ventured criticisms of *Captain Blood.* I half-knew that I was fuelling the fire; I suppose I hoped Flynn would break his neck in one of his flying leaps, or go on location to Tunisia. With the vogue for exotic costume pictures at the time, it was on the cards.

But I kept training and sparring with Spielberg, thinking that if I had to fight Flynn I should be as well prepared as possible. Larry was gentle with me in the ring and taught me more evasive tricks than aggressive moves. He knew that I was a pacifist at heart. Also that I was a good listener.

'Dick, I got a problem,' he said, during one of our running stints along the grey beach.

'So have I,' I gasped. 'I need to stop for a cigarette. All this seaweed air is killing me.'

'Just another half mile,' Larry said. His breath wouldn't have extinguished a kitchen match. 'It's Eben Cartwright and his cousin.'

I estimated the yardage to the pier – a quarter mile at least, maybe a half – far enough, anyway. I dug into my reserves of lung and leg strength for the distance. There wasn't much breath to spare for talking. 'What about 'em?'

'They look at me funny.'

The pier was getting closer but the sand was getting softer. 'Fighters have to live with that. People wonder how you do it.'

'It's not that. They look at me like I'm an animal or somethin'. And they never talk to me.'

My calves were cramping. 'Quote the Bible. That'll break the ice.' We reached the pier and I embraced one of the mussel-covered posts. 'Suffer the little children to come unto me,' I wheezed, dredging up ancient memories, 'or something such.'

'That's the New Testament, Dick. I'm a Jew. I don't know nothing about that stuff.'

'Forget them, Larry. They're just a couple of crazy rednecks. Harmless. When's your next fight?'

'November tenth, in San Diego. Some coloured guy. A ten rounder. When're you fighting Errol Flynn?'

See what I mean? There was no getting away from it. Larry knowing didn't mean they were talking about Browning vs Flynn down at the cannery (he'd probably picked something up from Belinda who used to kid around with him), but still, it was worrying. My only consolation was my fitness. If I couldn't out-fight Flynn, maybe I could out-run him. Strength came back into my legs right then, and I sucker-punched Larry lightly and shouted, 'Race you back to the car.' I gave myself a head-start and he only just beat me.

I showered at the gym and drove back to Casablanca thinking about Flynn, Belinda and my sinking bank balance. Mr Beer had refused to replace the gearbox on the Olds or buy new tyres and a new battery. I shelled out. Belinda's tastes were growing more expensive, and I needed New York clothes and London shoes if I was going to look the part I wanted to play. It all added up. Plus the fact that Eben Cartwright and Abel Buzzacott were getting seriously behind in their rent. So I had a lot on my mind when I pulled up in the driveway beside the house.

A man stepped out of the shadows as I opened the car door. 'Mr Browning?'

He was tall and well built and for a split second I thought it was Flynn. To do myself credit, I put up my fists – with the car keys between my fingers as a knuckle-duster. 'Who wants to know?'

'Take it easy, sir.' He flipped open a wallet and showed me a badge that suggested he was a member of a society that admired the American eagle. 'I'm Agent Peter Groom, FBI. I'd like to have a few words with you.'

'About what?'

'Let's get back in the car and take a ride.'

'Why?'

He kind of shooed me into the driver's seat and I obeyed meekly. Groom was pale-faced, like an easterner, and about thirty-five years old. He had a lean, disciplined look that commanded respect. He wore a light grey suit, hat to match. His shirt was discreetly striped, there was a neat gold pin holding down his plain tie, and you had to look hard to see the gun bulge under his left armpit. For no good reason I drove back to the beach.

Groom pointed to the parking lot behind the marina. It was almost deserted; a few seagulls were picking disappointedly at cigarette butts. 'This'll do.'

I pulled in and stopped, facing the flat, grey ocean. The sky was overcast with rain coming on. I lit a cigarette, and Groom wound his window down. I said, 'Let me see the buzzer again.'

He showed me the badge, which looked genuine. 'I can give you a number to ring where you can check my credentials, or we can go over to Burbank and I can introduce you to a few people. But I don't think all that's necessary, do you?'

He spoke in a harsh New England accent. He wore some kind of university insignia on his watch-chain, and everything else about him was right. If he wasn't FBI he was something else, possibly worse. 'No,' I said, 'that won't be necessary.'

He took out a notebook and turned the pages, which he covered with neat copperplate. 'We know quite a bit about you, Mr Browning. You entered this country as a seaman in 1919.'

'Legally,' I said.

'Of course. But then you really got around. I only have a summary here, but it seems you entered again from Mexico, and some time later from Canada. I don't think these other entries were quite as legal as the first.'

I smoked my Lucky down and didn't say anything.

'You were a principal in a firm known as Aussie Air. You might be regarded as an undischarged bankrupt. According to information from, ah . . ., I imagine you'll know the source, you were married in Australia.'

'Rupert MacKnight,' I said. 'That's your source.'

'Right. I'm glad to see we're communicating. That makes your marriage to Coral Smith in Red Springs, California in 1930 bigamous.'

This was getting too hot; I wanted a drink badly. 'How the hell did you find out about that?'

'Fingerprints. You don't have a valid work permit or a valid driver's licence. Did you have any trouble with the law back in Australia, Mr Browning?'

I threw my butt out for the seagulls – this was long before we heard of this nonsense about littering. 'Well, not . . .'

Groom shut his notebook. 'Of course you did, your type always does. We've got an awful lot on you, Mr Browning. Enough to shift you out of this country so fast your pants'd catch fire.'

I smelled a deal. I lit another cigarette. 'I'm not admitting anything. I want to consult my lawyer.'

'Who might that be?'

I floundered and reached back into my memory. 'Abe Kurtz of Red Springs.'

'Mr Kurtz was disbarred from the practice of law in 1932 for jury rigging. He's selling real estate now. You're in trouble.'

I drew on the cigarette and sucked the smoke down, trying to stay calm and work out what was going on. Everything Groom said was true, but was it worth the attention of the senior FBI man he appeared to be? That was the right question I felt sure. 'What do you want from me, Mr Groom?' I said.

He let out the sort of bark New Englanders use for a laugh. 'You're not as dumb as some folks think.'

'I hope not.'

'No, sir. Not dumb at all. And you're right, we *do* need something from you.'

'What?'

He held up his long, blue-veined hand and examined his wedding ring. 'Don't rush things. In return for your co-operation, I guarantee no action will be taken against you for your wanton violation of the laws of this country. You won't be deported, Mr Browning, or go to prison.'

It was the first mention of prison and Groom dropped it in just at the right moment. He had all my attention. 'What do you want?'

'Staying in your house are two men, Eben Cartwright and Abel Buzzacott. Correct?'

'Yes.'

'I have reason to believe that they are members of a clandestine organisation whose activities are not conducive to peace and harmony in society, especially *this* particular segment of society.'

'What segment?'

'The movie industry is an essential part of the fabric of American life.'

'What clandestine organisation?'

'I'm not going to tell you. I don't want you to make judgements or guesses. I just want you to get close to Cartwright and Buzzacott, get into their confidence. Can you do that?'

It sounded fairly harmless. 'Sure.'

'Good. I'll want reports from you on their statements and activities. How well do you know them as of now?'

'Not well. I collect their rent, when they pay it, which hasn't been too regular lately.'

The notebook came out. 'Have you ever heard them say anything unusual or suspicious.'

I began to regard the whole thing as a joke; it suddenly seemed very amusing to please a man who held a gold pen poised over an FBI notepad. 'Cartwright once said something about having a talk with me.'

'About what?'

'His principles.'

Groom scribbled. 'Good, that's good. You have that talk, Mr Browning, and let me know everything that's said.'

'Is that all?'

'By no means. I'm not offering you this amnesty for nothing. You have to go along with these men in whatever they may be doing, even if it's illegal. That's what undercover work is all about.'

'Illegal. You mean bank robbery and such?'

'I don't specify.'

'And are you offering me amnesty on that too? What if I get caught robbing a bank or kidnapping Daryl F. Zanuck's son?'

Groom settled back in his seat. 'In that event, we'd just have to see what we could do.'

CHAPTER TWENTY-THREE

It wasn't hard to start up a conversation with Eben Cartwright.

'Er, Eben, about the rent.'

'I'm sorry, Mr Browning,' Eben said, 'I'm temporarily short of funds.'

'I thought you taught school in East L.A.?'

'I quit. I've got a higher purpose.'

'You've got a higher rent, too. You're supposed to be paying for Abel's room, but I haven't had a cent. Does he have a job?'

'There's not much he's fitted to do, but he'll be my right-hand man when the time comes.'

'What time?'

Cartwright stared at me as if trying to read the secrets of my soul. 'I hope I can talk to you about that one day.'

We were standing on the ricketty balcony at the back of the house – the place where Belinda had first propositioned me. The view was nothing in particular, just houses, scruffy palm trees and a glimpse of the tops of the oil derricks. Eben shot the cuffs of the rather soiled shirt he wore under his black suit jacket and waved his hand at it all.

'What do you think of this place? This Los Angeles?'

'It's all right. You can make a living.'

'It's godless and soulless. It's run by . . . the wrong element. It's headed down the wrong road. And it could be so glorious! The movies that could be made here. Did you ever see *Birth of a Nation*, Mr Browning?'

'Well, a long time ago.'

'Now, there was a movie. I should just say it was. Am I right in thinking I heard you say on the telephone, pardon me for the intrusion, that you weren't a Catholic?'

A harmless religious nut, I thought. 'That's right.'

'And that you don't allow nigras in this house.'

I nodded.

Eben clapped me on the shoulder. 'That's good, that's good. I take it you'll be giving the Jew his marching orders pretty soon?'

'Eh?'

'The Jew. Spielberg. I assume you're learning boxing from him for your movie career. Fine sport boxing, as long as it's kept clean of the wrong element. When you've learned all you can from the Jew, you'll send him on his way.'

'I'm not sure about that,' I said with a bit of acid, 'he pays his rent.'

'Ah, the Hebrews always pay. But can they ever pay for what they once did? That's the question. Well, it was nice talking to you, sir.'

I felt I needed a little more to give to Groom, although I was pretty sure he'd be satisfied that Cartwright was a religious crazy, nothing more. I held the door open for Eben who almost bowed at the courtesy, but as if it was his due. 'You said something about your principles, Eben. I'd like . . .'

He turned to give me the soul-searching look again. His dark eyes were deep in the shadowed sockets – Universal could have used him in horror features. 'You're interested in my principles?'

'Yes.'

'Get rid of the Jew, and we'll talk again.'

I called the number Groom had given me, and he nominated a meeting place – a bridge over the sluggish Los Angeles river. We met there a few days later, and I gave him a full report on the conversation with Cartwright. He made a lot of notes and was impressed at my recall. I've always been able to remember conversations (if I've been sober at the time), I suppose because my mind isn't cluttered up with useless information.

'So you see,' I said, 'he's just a harmless crackpot. He and Abel're probably going to start one of those tinpot churches – the Church of the Bleeding Cross or some such rubbish.'

Groom, today in a light blue suit that set off the Californian tan he was starting to acquire, closed his notebook with a snap. 'He's far from harmless. You have to do it.'

'Do what?'

'Get rid of Spielberg in order to gain Cartwright's confidence.'

'But he's my friend.'

'Friendship sometimes has to be sacrificed to a higher good. In our organisation it happens every day.'

'You're sounding like him, like Eben.'

'Don't get me wrong, Browning. I'm not totally out of sympathy with Eben Cartwright's goals, but I have my orders and I'll carry them out, whatever my private feelings.'

'I wish I understood what was going on.'

Groom waved away a fly and took out his pocket handkerchief to dab at some sweat on his forehead. 'November, and it's still warm. It doesn't make sense.'

'Like what you're telling me to do.'

'Just do it, Browning, or you know the consequences.'

'What happened to the "Mr" before Browning?'

Groom tucked his handkerchief away and put his notebook back in his pocket. 'It doesn't do to be on too friendly terms with an informer. It makes for sloppiness. Ring the same number when you have something to report. This is very lucky for you. It's all working out very well.'

'Yeah, great,' I said. 'The same number. Isn't that a bit sloppy?'

'I'll decide what's sloppy, Browning. By the way, what's all this I hear about you and Errol Flynn? I'd say you were over-matched.'

'I don't understand, Dick.'

'I'm sorry, Larry. It's not me, it's Beer and the owner. They want to re-plaster and paint. Christ knows the place needs it.'

'Yeah, but why my room first? I gotta fight in three days. Why can't you start in Buzzacott's room? He could move in with his cousin for a coupla days.'

'I'm sorry, Larry. I'm just doing what I'm told.'

His hangdog look almost broke my heart, but survival is the strongest instinct of all. I helped Larry pack up his few things, clothes, boxing gear and his thin scrapbook, and drove him to the YMCA. He was silent and for him, with his usual sunny nature, sullen.

'It's those rednecks,' he said as he got out of the car. 'I know it is. They got it in for me 'cause I'm a Jew. Hell, half this town is Jews.'

I wanted to say something to comfort him and myself, to say he could come back when . . . but how could I? All I could do was shake his hand. 'I'll come to the fight, Larry. I'll be at ringside.'

'You'll see a fight. I'm mad.' He slung his bag across his shoulder and walked into the 'Y' leaving me feeling like the heel of the year.

The first person I saw back at Casablanca was Abel Buzzacott. He was carrying a cardboard box and coming out of Spielberg's room. I stopped him and said, 'What the hell are you doing?'

'Moving into the Jew's room. Eben said it'd be all right.'

'Did he?' I felt like kicking the buck-toothed little cretin down the stairs and only just stopped myself doing it. 'Well see about that.'

'Yup, Eben, he wants to see you too. He's out in the yard. Said to tell you.'

I ran down the stairs and went through the back door. Eben Cartwight was sawing some light wood into lengths. He put the saw down and held out his hand. 'I want to thank you, sir.'

I ignored the hand. 'You tricked me. You just wanted to get a better room for your half-wit cousin. Well, I'm not going to stand for it.'

'Don't fuss yourself. You'll understand when the time comes.'

'You keep talking about a time coming. What d'you mean? The goddamn second coming?'

'Don't blaspheme, Mr Browning. It isn't worthy of you. I'll make you a bargain – just you tell me a few things and I'll do the same.'

A hammer and nails were lying on the cement near the wood. I wanted to use the hammer on his head, but I could see Groom's gold pen and the blank pages of the notebook. I calmed down, promising myself a good shot of bourbon when I'd got what I needed from him. 'Shoot,' I said.

'They tell me you're from Australia. That right?'

I nodded.

'Your poppa and mama, where were they from?'

'Australia, born there. But I suppose you mean further back. Well, Ireland mostly, some Scottish in there, too.'

'That's fine. What's this White Australia policy I hear about?'

'It keeps out cheap labour. Australia's surrounded by Chinese and natives of one sort or another. If they were allowed in, the place'd be overrun by people who'd work for nothing.'

'You go along with that?'

I shrugged. 'Never thought much about it. I guess so.'

He grabbed my hand – no avoiding it this time – and shook it hard. 'Mister Browning, I got a very good feeling about you. I think we've got a lot in common. Some night soon I want you to meet a few friends of mine.'

'That's progress,' Groom said over the phone. 'That's real progress. You've got to play along.'

'It could be dangerous.'

'Not so sure he's harmless now, eh?'

'I don't know.'

'Only one sure way to find out.'

That night I drank, the next night I spent some time with Belinda, still looking over my shoulder at any tall, well set-up man who came into view. The night after that I went to the fights at the Figueroa. Larry Spielberg was in the ten-round wind-up before the main event. I cheered and yelled and won some money as Larry pounded a slow light-heavy by the name of 'Reb' Claymore into jelly in five rounds. I tried to fight my way through the crowd to congratulate him, but either he didn't see me or he didn't want to. I left halfway through the main event and went home to drink a portion of my winnings.

'You're distressed, brother,' Eben Cartwright said to me next day.

It was on the tip of my tongue to say 'hangover' but I just nodded.

'There's a meeting tonight will lighten your soul. I want you to come.'

'What sort of meeting?'

'Its out of town a piece. I'd be glad if you could drive Abel and me.'

That was good and bad news. I have a general dislike of the country, which I feel is much more dangerous than the city – highways, muggers, policemen and all. Still, if I was in control of the transport, that was a safeguard, and I had no choice. 'I'll be happy to,' I said.

We set off soon after dark, driving north into the citrus orchard country in the valley. We drove along straight roads through the orchards, until we turned off onto a series of dirt roads running past small mixed farms that looked to be struggling to make a living. A quarter mile ahead, a man stood in the middle of the road swinging a lantern.

'Follow him,' Eben said.

The man left the road and walked down a track towards a small farmhouse. I followed the lantern light, and when the man made an angry signal I dipped my headlights. He indicated that I should park behind the house. I pretended not to understand and parked where I could turn easily and quickly if I had to.

Eben opened the door, stepped out and shook the lantern-swinger's hand. 'Judd,' he said.

Groom had told me to memorise as many names and faces as possible. I started with Judd who was a tall, thin individual with ears that stuck straight out from his head. We went into the farmhouse, which was essentially a one-room shack with burlap curtains serving to petition off a couple of beds along one side of the room. There was a lantern hanging from a beam like the one that had been used to signal on the road. Three men were sitting around a table, not speaking. They stood up when Eben Cartwright entered.

'Sit down, brothers,' Eben said. 'Judd, hang up the lantern so we can all get a good look at our new brother here.'

I stood on the dirt floor feeling foolish while they looked at me and I looked at them: hard, country faces, yellow teeth, home haircuts and work clothes. Eben rattled off names, but I can't recall any of them, only Judd.

'Pretty smooth feller,' one of them said.

'He's with us,' Eben said, taking a seat at the table and gesturing for me to do the same. Abel Buzzacott stood by the door. 'He hates niggers and kikes, just like we do. Where he comes from, they don't even allow niggers into the country. Isn't that right, brother?'

I nodded.

'Powerful good idea,' another man muttered. 'We useta have 'em under control in Calhoun county, but now . . .' He shook his head regretfully and other heads moved in sympathy.

I knew it was time for me to do something. I took out a pocketknife and began carving my initials into the rough deal table. 'Niggers and Jews'll take this country over if white folks don't do something about it,' I said. 'It ain't my country, I'm from Australia like brother Eben says, but since I've been privileged to be here I've found that America is the greatest country on God's green earth. My folks hail from Ireland which is the greenest country on God's green earth . .' I was running out of steam and sense. I drew a breath and stuck the knife half an inch into the table top. 'I swear I can't stand to see the niggerfication and kikification of this sweet land of milk and honey.'

To a man, they stood up and cheered. They clapped me on the back and said what a fine fellow I was.

'By God, Eben,' Judd said, 'we got us a real firebrand here.'

Cartwright smiled broadly. 'Sure we have. I knew you boys'd be impressed. Brother Richard is the key to our success at this place in time.'

I pulled the knife out of the table and went on with my carving. 'What do you mean, Eben?'

We have all sworn an oath,' Cartwright said. 'An oath you will swear, too . . .'

'Hold hard, brother,' one of the men said. 'We don't know much about this feller. He talks good but. . .'

Cartwright didn't like being interrupted. 'This man acts,' he snapped, 'he turns niggers and other trash away from his establishment, and he took my advice and ee-jected a Jew was living there.'

The unconvinced one opened his mouth. 'Why. . .'

'He was learning boxing from the Jew,' Cartwright said. 'You understand? He was hitting the Jew with his fists!'

There was some muttering around the table about Jews and boxing and niggers. . . Max Baer, Joe Louis. One of the men sucked his yellow teeth and applied to Cartwright for permission to speak. Eben gave him the floor.

'Got me jest one question, Eben. I thought this was an American outfit.'

'I'm on my way to being an American,' I said. 'But what you're in here is a worldwide fight. There's a guy in Germany name of Hitler feels the same way we do, and let me tell you I've been in places where they do things right. Any of you ever been to South Africa?'

Heads were shaken.

'By God, they do it right there. The word for a nigger in South Africa is *munt,* that means a pile of . . . excrement.'

'That's in the Bible!' Judd shouted.

The doubters fell silent. Abel Buzzacott said grace and we had coffee and biscuits. A Bible was produced and preparations were made for my swearing-in. I was asked to wait in the lean-to kitchen at the back of the shack. I stood in the darkness listening to what sounded like a trunk being opened, and then the rustling of cloth. After a time Cartwright called, 'Come in, brother.'

I went back into the room. The five men were standing in a line with their arms folded across their chests. They wore white robes that completely covered their bodies. On their heads were high peaked cloth hoods with slits cut in them for the eyes and mouth.

CHAPTER TWENTY-FOUR

I don't remember much about the mumbo-jumbo that followed – it was all to do with the Bible and brotherhood and swearing on parts of the anatomy of live and dead mothers. I did my part, intoning away and rolling my eyes like the best of them. I was only thankful that there was no mixing of blood – I wouldn't have cared to risk taking on the mental and physical disabilities of that bunch. After the oath-taking there were more prayers and more coffee and cake. I was dying for a drink and a cigarette, but there was no alcohol on the premises and, although a couple of them smoked pipes, I got the feeling that they regarded cigarettes as instruments of the devil. In that they were right, of course.

Eben, Abel and I pushed off around midnight.

'Great bunch of fellers,' I said, hoping to have my memory refreshed about a few names, 'especially that tall guy with the squint. Ah . . .'

Neither of them volunteered a name. Eben spoke only to give me directions; Abel sat in the back sniffing, hawking and spitting out the window.

Eben sent Abel off to bed as soon as we reached the house. There was something strange about his movements. He didn't act towards me like a brother who'd just sworn an eternal oath of loyalty, secrecy and all the rest. As for me, I was anxious to get the night over.

'Well, it's been interesting, Eben. I'll just say goodnight now.'

'Come up to my room, and let's talk a spell.'

'It's late.'

He took hold of my arm. His fingers were surprisingly strong, and short of punching him out then and there, I had no alternative. We sat on the bed in his room under a fly-speckled light. There were several photographs tacked to the walls over the patches of peeling plaster and paint – family groups and church congregations, and one or two of men with spade beards and women in neck-to-knee dresses.

'Well, Mr Browning, what did you make of our little gathering?'

'I'm all for it,' I said. 'The Ku Klux Klan is the conscience of this country. It. . .'

'Hush. We're not what you'd call a properly constituted chapter of the Klan. Not yet. That's what this's all about.'

'Oh?'

His deep-buried eyes took on a glow that was almost reddish, mad-looking anyway. 'I'm aiming to be affiliated. I'm aiming to make the Klan a power in this part of the world. To do that we have to make some folks in the south sit up and take notice. Do you follow me?'

'Er, not exactly, Eben.'

He whacked his bony fist into the palm of the other hand with a noise like a pistol shot. 'We have to do something! Something to get their attention. Give some of those lazy Grand Wizards in Georgia and Louisiana the message that here in Los Angeles the fight is on!'

I tried to look enthusiastic. I nodded vigorously and did some fist-whacking of my own.

'We'll get funds and supporters. We can organise, reach into the schools and churches. We can grow!'

'Magnificent,' I said, 'but what can we do? What?'

Suddenly, the light died in his eyes. 'Do you think I'm a fool, Mr Browning?'

'No, Eben, of course not.'

'I know you're an actor, sir. Maybe you're a pretty good one. Anyway, it's hard to tell when an actor's acting and when he isn't. Right?'

'Yes, but. . .'

He patted my knee. 'Just don't fuss yourself. I trust you and I've got me a little insurance as well. That's the way this business works. Take Abel for an instance. Now he's strong in the faith, but just in case he isn't, I know things he did back in Georgia that'd put him in the prison farms, choppin' weeds an' diggin' ditches, for the rest of his days. And he knows I know. I'd never tell, 'course I wouldn't, but it never hurts to have a strong grip on a man.'

'I see. But you've got nothing on me.'

'What if I was to tell Larry Spielberg's buddies at the cannery that you threw him out of this house on account of he was a dirty Jew?'

My jaw dropped; the dark eyes were searching my face like raking spotlights. It was a mild night, but I started to shiver.

'But, as I say, don't worry. I'm sure you're with us all the way, and there's grand things ahead. When they make a real movie about the Klan, a true movie, well, I leave it to your imagination who'll be in line for the major roles.'

It sounds ridiculous now, of course, and a silly thought crossed my mind as he spoke. *You'll need blacks and Jews to play niggers and kikes,* but, sitting there in that bare bedroom with Eben Cartwright, it was more terrifying than funny. He took out his fob watch and checked the time.

'It's late,' he said, 'but not too late to tell you exactly what we're going to do.'

I met Groom two days later in a bar in Santa Monica. It seemed that I'd spent a lot of those forty-eight hours in bars. 'They're going to plant fiery crosses on the front lawns of selected Jews.'

'Who?'

I was half-drunk and angry. 'Haven't you been listening? These crazy would-be Ku Klux Klansmen.'

Groom sipped his lemonade; he was the type to regret the repeal of the Volsted Act. 'I meant, which Jews?'

'I want another drink.'

'You've had enough.' Groom took out his notebook and gold pen. 'You're almost there, Mr Browning . . .'

'So it's "Mr Browning" again, is it?'

'It can be. Names, please.'

'Selznick, Zukor, Goldwyn, Mayer. . . everybody.'

'When?'

'Starting tomorrow night.'

'Who's first?'

'Mayer. God help me, I'm supposed to drive them around. They've got these wooden crosses wrapped with rags. They're going to soak the rags in gasoline. Madness. All right Mr G-man, how're you goin' to stop 'em?'

'We're not going to stop them. At least, not until they've got one of the crosses well and truly burning. Will they be wearing the robes?'

'Sure, but. . .'

'Where does Mayer live?'

'In Bel Air. The big moment's set for 11 p.m. Lunatics, the lot of them!'

'Great, that's just great. You've done this country a great service, Mr Browning, or you will have by the time tomorrow night's over.'

'You want me to play along?'

Groom nodded. 'Right up until we move in.'

'Then what happens?'

'We'll look after you. Will you do it?'

'What choice do I have? I'll do it on one condition?'

'Which is?'

'That you buy me another bloody drink.'

In a way, it's comforting to have no alternative courses of action. If I didn't play along with Cartwright, he'd set Larry Spielberg's fish cannery mates on me; if I didn't play along with Groom I'd go to prison or be deported or both. I had to do what I had to do. Comforting, but not very. After Groom left I spent the rest of the day drinking in the bar. Around eight, I drove to Culver City (God knows how I got there, the other drivers must've all avoided me), to find consolation in the arms of Belinda Douglas.

Consolation wasn't what Belinda was all about. Parked outside her apartment building was a big, white Cadillac convertible with the top down. I stood and looked at it for a long time and must have sobered up enough to climb the stairs quietly. Belinda's windows were open and the sounds that were coming from inside were very familiar. When she made love Belinda had a way of grunting faster and faster as she experienced the pleasure all through her body. From the pitch she was at just then, I calculated she was feeling it in her knees.

I re-negotiated the stairs and went back to the Cadillac. A lot of drinking gives you one capacity in particular. I eased open the driver's door of the Caddy, unbuttoned and emptied my very full bladder all over the white leather upholstery. It made me feel better, not as good as Belinda was feeling maybe, but better than her boyfriend would be feeling when he sat down to drive home.

CHAPTER TWENTY-FIVE

I slept around the clock and felt like hell when I woke up the following afternoon. Just in case something had changed, or there was an
angle I'd missed, I reviewed my options while I stood in the shower
for twenty minutes. I came out clean, refreshed but still, as they say
now, between a rock and a hard place. I ate something and drank
coffee. I smoked. My stomach was twitching, and I made frequent
trips to the bathroom. Duluth was back in gaol, I was alone in the
house with Cartwright and Buzzacott. Several times I went outside
and contemplated disabling the car. But where would that get me?
They'd probably send me out to steal another one.

Some time after nine, Judd arrived carrying a parcel wrapped in
brown paper. You didn't have to be a Harvard man to guess what it
was. Eben called me up to his room and we did some praying. I have
to admit that I felt I could use all the help I could get. To myself, I
changed the words of the prayers from 'prosper our enterprise' and
'aid us in our cause' to 'don't let there be any shooting' and 'please,
please let me get out of this mess'. I got some genuine help in the
form of a few stiff shots of bourbon. If Eben noticed, he didn't say
anything. Maybe he didn't notice; the gasoline can we loaded into
the trunk of the Oldsmobile, along with the rag-wrapped cross,
leaked a little and made the car smell like a Molotov cocktail.

Abel unwrapped the bedsheet robes and hoods and put them
lovingly on the back seat of the car.

I'm doing the driving, right?' I said, 'no need for me to wear a robe.'

'You'll wear one,' Cartwright said. 'Let's go, brothers.'

We took Venice Boulevard east and went north on La Brea to Bel Air. Abel Buzzacott and Judd sat in the back. Cartwright was ice cool beside me, telling me occasionally to slow down and tch-tching when I drove badly and nervously, which was often. It was a fine night, which was bad luck. If it had been pouring as it sometimes is in Southern California at that time of year, they wouldn't have been able to light the crosses. No such luck. No flat tyres, no cops stopping to ask to see my non-existent driver's licence. No earthquake.

These days, non-residents found in Bel Air are likely to be strip-searched by security guards every block or kept under surveillance from a helicopter, but back then it was just a place in the lower reaches of the mountains where rich people lived in big houses. Mayer's place had a fairly narrow frontage for the area, not more than a hunded yards, and the house was set fairly close to the road. The shaven, manicured lawn in front wouldn't have been much bigger than a football field.

'What in the name of the Lord Jesus is going on here?' Cartwright stared at the gleaming cars parked in rows on the broad driveway that led to the house. The house itself, a sort of miniature castle in white, was all lit up.

'A party,' I said, feeling relief flood through me. 'They're having a party. We'll have to call it off.'

'A Jew party,' Cartwright bit the words off and spat them out. 'Couldn't be better. Let them all see the wrath of the Lord.'

'But there's bound to be people around, guys parking the cars, guests arriving . . .'

'Hebrews and flunkeys,' Cartwright said. 'Besides, Abel's got the text for the occasion. Haven't you, Abel?'

I turned around and saw Abel struggling into his robe. Lying beside him on the seat was a sawn-off shotgun.

'My god,' I said.

'Is stronger than theirs.' Cartwright handed me a hood, and the nightmare began in earnest. Judd took the cross and soaked it in gasoline. He rattled a box of matches in his pocket under the robe and wiggled the wooden mallet.

'Ready,' he said.

We crouched behind the car, four men in white robes with twenty-five yards to cover to reach the garden shrubs and another twenty-five to the centre of the lawn. No front fence. We scuttled into the thick, scented bushes. From there, I could hear the sound of music from the house. I stared through the darkness at the bright windows and saw figures moving behind them. I peered to left and right, but I didn't see Peter Groom. I didn't expect to. Maybe it would suit his purpose to let a couple of crosses burn before he nabbed Cartwright. I wished I'd known about the shotgun.

Cartwright hissed, 'Let's do it!' and he took off across the lawn, running like a rabbit despite the flapping robe. I felt the shotgun dig me in the spine and I followed, hot and sweating under the cloth and feeling the hood slip down over my eyes. I stumbled and almost fell. Then the shotgun slammed into my back again, and I stopped. I heard the mallet hitting the top of the cross. I struggled to pull the slit holes into a place where I could look through them. Then I heard the match strike and the whoosh of the gasoline igniting.

'Stand where you are!' The voice was Groom's and very close. I was the first to raise my hands.

The shotgun boomed close to my ear, and I finally managed to see. The cross was burning fiercely; Abel Buzzacott was crouched, working the action of the shotgun. Three sharp shots sounded and I felt the heat of them as they whipped past my ear.

'Don't shoot! Don't shoot!' It's me!' I yelled. I clawed off the hood, lifted the skirts of the robe and sprinted for the house. Heat from the burning cross seared me as I rushed past it. I heard more shooting behind me and some screaming. I saw people coming from the front of the house, and I swerved to the side and dashed along a paved walkway under a vine-covered pergola. It was dark here, but not as dark as it should have been. I seemed to be carrying light with me. I looked down and saw that the right sleeve of the robe was on fire. I yelled and beat at it with the hood. I stopped running and tore the robe to shreds trying to get out of it. Finally I got it off and stamped out the last sparks. I leaned against the oiled wood of the pergola, panting with terror and wondering what to do next. There was shouting behind me, and I instinctively moved away from the noise and found myself halfway along the side of the house where a balcony jutted out from a brightly-lit room.

I climbed over the rail and went into the room. There was a long table laid with party food and party drinks. I grabbed a bottle of champagne and upended it. I poured most of the chilled bottle down my throat and felt it hit me like a hailstorm. I was reaching for another bottle when I heard sounds nearby in the house, getting louder. I grabbed the bottle and ducked out of the room into a passage where paintings hung along the wall. I staggered past the Old Masters towards an oak-panelled door that had GAMES ROOM written on it in gold leaf. I pushed open the door and went into a softly-lit room that contained a gun rack, a bar and a pool table.

A man was standing at the bar pouring himself a drink. A tall man with broad shoulders inside a beautifully cut white linen suit. He turned around as he heard the door open. He smiled and raised the glass towards his impossibly white teeth.

'Well, what do you know,' he said. 'I'm very pleased to meet up with you at last, sport.'

I leaned back against the door and stared into the mocking grey eyes of Errol Flynn.

CHAPTER TWENTY-SIX

Why didn't I spin around, open the door and run? That would've been my normal reaction to a situation like this, but the situation was far from normal. The world had become an unfriendly place, full of Ku Klux Klansmen and federal agents and vengeful fish filleters. Although Errol Flynn was at least as tall as me, a few pounds heavier and fifteen years younger, I felt safer where I was. With luck, I'd be able to talk my way out of this. I extended the bottle of champagne I still held in my hand.

'Peace offering, sport,' I said. 'One Aussie to another.'

Flynn smiled and sipped his drink. 'Piss on your peace offering. An appropriate expression in this case, I think.'

'Don't follow you,' I said. 'Look, about this business of me running you down, calling you a poof and so on – it's all malarky.'

'I know it's malarky.' Flynn moved and I found myself edging away from him towards the pool table, where a couple of cues were sitting within reach. Trouble was, it gave Flynn space to get between me and the door, so that escape was cut off if I should decide that it was more dangerous in here after all.

'It was my agent's idea,' I babbled. 'Robert Silkstein. If you knew Robert you'd understand. He dreamed it up as a way of getting publicity for me.'

'I know Robert. He's a sneaking, lying son of a bitch, and so are you, Browning.'

'Fair go. We Aussies should stick together.'

Flynn drained his drink. There was a slight flush in his cheeks, and I realised that it hadn't been his first. Perhaps if I could keep him talking he'd have a few more and pass out. But he put his glass down on a chair and appeared to lose interest in drinking.

'I didn't mind too much when I heard the stories about how you'd were going to sort me out,' he said. 'I understand about publicity. I came here as an Olympic boxing medal winner, which I'm not.'

'Heard about it,' I said. 'Good stunt that, who dreamed it up? I . . .'

'Mind you, I'm not saying I *couldn't* have won a medal for boxing. I like a good fight.'

'Mm.' I was over by the table now, and I put the bottle on the edge. My hand rested near a pool cue. 'I hear you work out with Mushy Callahan.'

'Among others. I fought in Sharman's[37] tents at home a few times.'

'Is that a fact? Hey, what're you doing?'

He was moving a heavy chair across and wedging it against the door. He peeled off his jacket and draped it over the chair. Then he took off his tie, unfastened his cuffs and rolled up his sleeves. 'I don't want any interruptions.'

I circled away. 'I thought we were going to talk this out. You said you understood about the publicity angle.'

'Oh, I do, old son. But that's not why I'm going to beat the shit out of you.'

I abandoned the idea of grabbing a pool cue. He could probably use one as a sword to put my eye out or as a quarter staff to crack my skull. 'Why, then?'

'Because you pissed all over the front seat of my Cadillac, you dirty bastard.'

Don't think it was my outraged sense of honour that made me roll up my sleeves and get ready to fight Errol Flynn. Given the way Flynn and Belinda approached life, it was only a matter of time before they ended up in bed together. Nor was it the threat from outside; I was dimly aware of commotion beyond the walls of the games room, but only dimly. Fact is, I still don't know why I did it. For the first time in my life I wanted to fight. I must have been in a very precarious emotional state. The bottle of champagne inside me probably helped.

I shaped up to Flynn and surprised him by getting him on the nose with a long left that snapped his head back.

His counter was a short right to the ribs that took my breath away. I backed off and he came at me too confidently, wide open. I swung from a crouch and got him above the heart. He grunted and missed me with a hook. At that point, I'd say I was winning, but from then on it was hard to say. Flynn could box all right and hit hard, and do both of those things better than me, but I had one advantage over him – I didn't have to protect my good looks. For all his footwork and combinations, all his fast jabs and tasty hooks, he was partly on the defensive, worried about the shape of his nose. I waded in, taking punishment, trying to land on or near the elegant nose and gleaming teeth. He could see what I was doing, and he didn't like it. He hit me hard and often but, and I have to say this, fairly. Neither of us went below the belt, don't ask me why. We knocked over the champagne bottle and broke a few glasses but fought only with fists. The alcohol and desperation must have dulled the pain. I knocked him down a couple of times and felt the skin tear on my knuckles. He knocked me flat about as often, then stood back and waited for me to get up. I expected a kick from his highly polished wingtip shoes, but they stayed firmly planted on the floor. As a fighter, Errol Flynn was a gentleman.

We must have been at it for half an hour or more, getting weary and doing some pushing and shoving as well as punching. My hands were sore and my arms ached. I could hardly lift them to block punches, let alone throw them. Flynn was in about the same condition. His silk shirt was torn to shreds, and my work shirt was a sopping wet rag. We stood toe-to-toe in the middle of the room and slugged. I got him on the mouth and split his lip. He pounded me again in the ribs where it felt like a hole was opening up.

Then there was shouting and banging, and the door was shoved open. The chair skidded across the room, cannoned into us and knocked us both down. A dozen men and women burst into the room, which was a shambles of upturned furniture, broken glass, torn curtains and sprayed blood. I saw Mayer's outraged look as he surveyed his games room, and I recognised a couple of other big-wigs – Selznick, I think, and Sam Goldwyn. Peter Groom was there too, immaculate as always but no gun or badge in sight.

'What the hell is going on here?' Mayer said.

Flynn and I used the back of the same chair to haul ourselves up simultaneously. 'Little fight between friends,' Flynn said. 'Pay for the damage.'

Goldwyn elbowed his way forward. 'Fighting?' he said. 'I like a good fight. Fight some more.'

I looked at Flynn. His face was swollen and his mouth was split and puffed. I was looking through half-closed eyes and holding my ribs together by sheer willpower. We both shook our heads.

'Who's winning?' Goldwyn said.

Flynn and I spoke simultaneously. 'A draw,' we said.

Someone came and took Flynn away, and apologised to Mayer and said I'd pay for my share of the damage. Peter Groom stepped forward and showed Mayer his badge.

'This man has performed a very brave act, Mr Mayer. But for him, we would never have caught the men who perpetrated that atrocity on your lawn.'

'That's good enough for me,' Mayer said. 'Forget the damage, I never use the goddamn room anyway.'

Groom helped me to a bathroom. I asked him what had happened, and he told me that Cartwright had been shot dead and that Judd and Abel Buzzacott were in custody.

'What about me? Those crazies'll try to land me in the shit with them.'

Groom shook his sleek head. 'You've wiped the slate, Mr Browning.'

'Good,' I said, and then I passed out cold before I could get cleaned up.

CHAPTER TWENTY-SEVEN

I woke up in a hospital bed, which is something I never like to do. The room was dim, and my first panicky thought was that I'd been seriously injured somehow without knowing it at the time. Slowly I checked myself over: I found that I could see and hear and move everything. I knew there had been no blows below the belt, so I had no fears on *that* score. I had an almighty pain in my left side though, and my hands were bandaged. When I say I could see, I mean only just – my eyes were still banged up and the bones and flesh around them were tender. Still, I felt pretty good. I'd gotten clear of the Klan, was in good with the FBI, and I'd fought a fifteen-round draw with Errol Flynn.

The hospital routine got going – noisy trolleys in the corridor, breezy nurses rousing grumpy patients, and lukewarm coffee arriving with soggy toast. I had difficulty in drinking and eating, but I managed bravely. I asked a nurse who'd brought me in.

'Gary Cooper,' she said.

'Who?'

She was a pretty little thing with big brown eyes that were only for me at that moment. 'Don't you remember? You were at a party, and you got into a fight. Who did you fight, Gary Cooper?'

'No,' I said, 'Errol Flynn.'

She didn't believe me, and the magic was shattered. I dozed for a while and when I woke up another nurse was taking my pulse.

'What's wrong with me?'

She let go of my wrist and wrote something on the bed chart. 'Doctor will see you soon,' she said.

The doctor was an old, wheezy guy who looked like a country vet. He peered into my slitted eyes and consulted the chart. 'How're ya feelin'?'

'Sore.'

'Not surprised. You've got two cracked ribs. How's the other guy?'

'He lost some blood.'

Wish I coulda seen it. Well, we've got you all taped up and given you some shots. You can go home tomorrow. Someone to see you. You up to it?'

I nodded, and they ushered Belinda in. She was wearing red and white and looked fresh and pure. If I knew her, she'd leave the hospital in a nurse's uniform. But I was feeling at peace with the world, so I let her kiss me and make a fuss. I didn't say anything about her two-timing me with Errol Flynn. She left, after fifteen minutes, declaring her love, leaving fruit and flowers and talking about a weekend at Malibu. I think the plan included me.

Then the bedside telephone rang. I reached for it and squealed as the movement hurt my side. But I got the receiver off the hook and said hello.

'That you, sport? Flynn here. How're you feeling?'

I drew in a deep breath. 'If you're sitting by a swimming pool with a drink in one hand and some woman's tit in the other, I'm feeling lousy.'

He laughed. 'No fear. I'm in hospital, same as you. It was a draw, wasn't it? What's the damage?'

'Cracked ribs. You?'

'Hairline jaw fracture, you bastard, plus two loose teeth and a split lip. My hands are a mess.'

'Mine too.'

'Great, wasn't it? We must do it again some time, maybe for charity.'

'Yes, sure,' I said, meaning no way in the bloody world. 'Belinda been in to see you?'

He sounded genuinely puzzled. 'Belinda?'

Well, that was Flynn. We talked for ten minutes or so, about home and the movies and what was coming up for him and how it might be fun to work together. He did most of the talking while I said 'Yes' and 'Sure' and tried to work out whether he was kidding or not.

'My jaw's hurting, old son, better give it a rest. We'll have a few snorts together soon, what do you say?'

'Sure,' I said, 'your shout.'

He laughed and rang off. I lay for a while thinking about what he'd said. It sounded like a big break to me; I only hoped I didn't have to fight him again to stay in his good books. A bit later a trolley came around with newspapers and magazines. I bought the *Examiner* and read about the 'incident at the home of movie mogul Louis B. Mayer'. An FBI spokesman said an undercover agent had led a dangerous gang of fanatics to expose themselves. One of the fanatics was dead, and two others were charged with wounding (a Federal agent had been shot), trespass and breach of the peace.

Then the door opened and N. Robert Silkstein came in. I realised that it was the first time I had ever seen him outside his own office. In the hospital room he looked smaller and much less sure of himself. He pulled a chair up to the bed. I kept my eyes nearly closed which wasn't difficult.

'Kid,' he said softly. 'Kid, can you hear me?'

I let him wait for a few minutes before I opened one battered peeper. 'Hullo, Robert.'

He reached into his breast pocket. 'Kid, I got your earnings here on the Warners' picture.'

'Thanks, Robert. Just leave it on the bed. Sorry I can't talk much, I'm very tired.'

He leaned closer. I smelled the aftermath of Havana cigars and French aftershave. 'Kid,' he whispered, 'you did great. Just great. And it's gonna pay off.'

'I'm glad you're happy. Pay off how?'

'Keep it under your hat, but I think I can get you into the biggest thing that's gonna come out of this town. I mean ever.'

'What's that?'

'*Gone with the Wind,* what else?'

I closed my eyes. 'I don't want to be in Gone with the bloody Wind. It's a sure-fire turkey. I want to be in *Santa Fe Trail* with Flynn and Ronnie Reagan.'

***

APPENDIX

THE RELIABILITY OF FILM STAR MEMOIRS

It is not necessary to go all the way with Browning's view that 'all movie star biographies are crap' (p. 122) to be aware that as historical records these sorts of books have to be approached with caution. Two incidents touched on by Browning in this account of his third sojourn in Hollywood illustrate the point.

David Niven's two books of reminiscence, *The Moon's a Balloon* (1971) and *Bring on the Empty Horses* (1975) became best-sellers and are widely regarded as frank and factual accounts. Yet in the two books Niven gives quite different accounts of the same incident (an incident that was of significance to Browning).

Speaking of working with Errol Flynn on *The Charge of the Light Brigade,* Niven comments that Flynn was disliked by the extras for his arrogance. He continues:

> They were a rough lot too, the toughest of the riders from the Westerns, plus the stunt men who specialised in galloping falls. Flynn, they decided, had a swollen head, having made too big a success too soon . . .
>
> One day they were lined up on the parade ground of our fort, somewhere in the San Fernando Valley. Flynn and I were slightly in front of our men when one of them leaned

forward with his lance, rubber-tipped to cut down accidents, and wriggled it in Flynn's charger's dock.

The animal reared up and Flynn completed the perfect parabola and landed on his back.

Six hundred very muscular gentlemen roared with laughter.

Flynn picked himself up. 'Which one of you sons of bitches did that?'

'I did, sonny,' said a huge gorilla of a man, 'want to make anything of it?'

'Yes, I do,' said Flynn. 'Get off your horse.'

Nobody could stop it and the fight lasted a long time. At the end of it the 'gorilla' lay flat on his back. After that everyone liked Errol a lot more.

(*The Moon's a Balloon*, Coronet Ed., p. 180)

In Niven's later account, instead of simply sitting on his horse, Flynn 'let his reins go slack and busied himself with mirror and comb before a "close-up".' Now, the 'gorilla' is 'a large broken-nosed character' and instead of the fight lasting a long time, Flynn's opponent 'was taken to the Infirmary ten minutes later.' (*Bring on the Empty Horses,* Coroneted. pp. 105–6.)

Flynn's own brief account of the filming of this picture in his autobiography (*My Wicked, Wicked Ways,* London, 1960, Pan ed. pp. 184-5) makes no mention of the incident and is mainly devoted to the bad conditions under which the actors worked, and the cruel treatment of the horses.

The director John Huston, a noted boxer in his youth, gives an account of a fight he had with Errol Flynn. It occurred at a party in David O. Selznick's house:

Errol must have been spoiling for trouble . . . for he very quickly got around to saying something wretched about someone – a woman in whom I'd once been very interested and still regarded with deep affection. I was furious at his remark, and I said, "That's a lie! Even if it weren't a lie, only a sonofabitch would repeat it." Errol asked if I'd like to make anything out of it, and I decided that I would. Errol led the way and we went down to the bottom of the garden – just the two of us. No one knew we'd left the party.

According to Huston, he and Flynn fought for almost an hour, until the party broke up. He credits Flynn with being a good and fair fighter. Huston's recollection is that the fight was fair, but the language was foul. Flynn suffered two broken ribs and Huston a broken nose, cut eye and damage to his elbows. (John Huston, *An Open Book,* Macmillan, London, 1981, pp. 97–8).

Again, David Niven's account is substantially different:

John Huston . . . liked a good punch-up now and then. On one famous occasion, he and Flynn decided that they were bored at a Hollywood soiree. 'Tell you what, kid,' said Huston. 'Let's get the hell outa here and go down to the bottom of the garden and just mix it a little. Whaddya say?'

'You're on!' said Flynn.

(Bring on the Empty Horses, p. 107)

Errol Flynn makes no mention of the fights with Huston and Browning; perhaps he had so many that no single one stood out in his memory.

In this context, Browning's account of incidents that occurred while *The Plainsman* was being filmed can be seen as additional touches on the fast-fading historical record. The autobiographical accounts of Anthony Quinn and Cecil B. De Mille differ slightly, but significantly, in their treatment of the famous episode in which

Quinn impersonated a Cheyenne Indian.[39] In general, Browning's account is close to Quinn's, reflecting their common status as bit players. In some respects, Quinn's memory is faulty. He records wearing an 'old torn shirt' in his celebrated scene but in the film he is bare-chested. On other points, however, he is accurate. Quinn says, 'I looked over and there was a man dressed just like me, with the same make-up.' That man, we now know, was Richard Browning.

NOTES

1. See *Browning Takes Off.*
2. New Jersey's Mickey Walker fought three hundred bouts between 1905 and 1930. He held the world welterweight and middleweight titles and fought successfully in the top ranks of the light-heavyweight and heavyweight divisions.
3. Browning's reckoning is fairly accurate. Geronimo died in 1909, but his military operations had ceased in 1886. See *Geronimo: his own story,* ed. S.M. Barrett, (London, 1924).
4. Browning uses the word in the American sense, referring to what Australians and the British call scones.
5. Strictly, a 'sweetback man' is a pimp, one who lives off the earnings of a prostitute, but by extension any apparently lazy man who seems to be supported by a working woman.
6. For Browning's association with Clara Bow, see *'Beverly Hills' Browning,* p. 174–7; for Belinda Douglas, see later in this book.
7. Browning's memory seems amiss here. The expression 'race riot' was not in use in the 1930s.
8. The Empire State Building on 5th Avenue between 33rd and 34th Streets was built in 1930-31.
    At 102 storeys, it was for many years the tallest building in the world.
9. For Browning's experiences in Mexico, see *'Beverly Hills' Browning,* chaps. 6-13.

PETER CORRIS

10. Yass is a town approximately 33 kilometres south-west of Sydney.
11. *King Kong* was remade in 1976. There have been two Japanese spin-offs, *King Kong vs Godzilla* (1963) and *King Kong Escapes* (1968). In *King Kong Lives* (1986) the giant ape is revived and provided with a mate and offspring.
12. The geek was a circus performer, typically alcoholic or mentally deficient, who bit the heads off live chickens.
13. Browning refers to the kidnap and murder in the 1930s of the infant son of famous aviator Charles Lindbergh.
14. Primo Carnera was world heavyweight champion from 1932 to 1934; he was succeeded by Max Baer, who lost the title to James Braddock one year later.
15. See *'Box Office' Browning*, p. 123.
16. Owen 'Owney' Madden was a Liverpuddlian who migrated to the United States as a child. After a violent, criminal youth he was sentenced to 10 to 20 years for the murder of another gangster. He was released in 1923 and continued a career in crime as a union heavy and hijacker, but with a lower profile. He was gaoled briefly in 1932 for parole violation and quit the rackets shortly after. He died in 1964 of natural causes.
17. In 1934 Butte's mineral industry was disrupted by a series of long, bitterly fought strikes. See Joseph H. Howard (ed.), *Montana: high, wide and handsome,* (New Haven, 1959), p. 100.
18. Browning is close: Joe Louis won the fight in the third round.
19. As a New Deal measure, jobs were created with the Montana State Park Authority. Officers responsible for the preservation of forests were popularly known as the 'tree army'.
20. See *Browning Takes Off,* chaps 12–14.

21. For Browning's association with Douglas Fairbanks, see *'Beverly Hills' Browning* chaps. 16–22. Arthur Rosson was born in England, and came to America as a child. He worked as a goldminer in Nevada and briefly on the stage before becoming a stunt man and bit player. He wrote and directed numerous silent films but with the coming of sound he worked chiefly as a production manager and assistant director. His two brothers Richard and Hal also worked in movies, as a director and cinematographer. Hal Rosson was the last husband of Jean Harlow.

22. 'Stoush' is Australian slang for a fight.

23. Erich Von Stroheim was famous for his extravagance in the mounting of the films he directed. He is said to have ordered silk underwear for a thousand extras in a costume picture because the feel of wearing silk would add conviction to the extras' movements, see Budd Schulberg, *Moving Pictures,* (New York, 1981), pp. 219–50.

24. See *Browning Takes Off,* pp. 171–2.

25. Charlie Stevens was said to be a grandson of Geronimo. He made a career of playing villainous, frequently drunken, Indians in Westerns.

26. See *Browning Takes Off,* pp. 157–60.

27. Ned Kelly, an Australian outlaw hanged in 1880 for the murder of several policemen, is reputed to have said 'Such is life' on the scaffold.

28. Browning is wrong in saying that the film has a happy ending. Hickok is shot dead, although it is implied that frontier civilisation progresses.

29. See Appendix for a discussion of Browning's account of these events.

30. 'School' is an Australian expression for a group of gamblers or drinkers.

31. See *Browning Takes Off,* pp. 171–2.

32. Browning does not precisely locate the house, and Columbia Drive has been much developed since the 1930s. It has not been possible to identify 'Casablanca'. The difficulty in questioning old residents on the matter is that they confuse the name of the house with the film.

> Several of Browning's photographs from this period survive, but they are of very poor quality. Some show a big, white stucco house in the background but provide no useful locating clues. Similarly, the faces of the groups of men and women are faded beyond recognition. Nor do the hastily scrawled initials on the back help. Browning was not an assiduous memorabiliast.

33. James Murray experienced some brief success in movies in the 1920s and 1930s but his career failed to prosper, possibly due to his alcoholism. He committed suicide in 1936. Cornell Woolrich wrote hundreds of stories for pulp magazines and a series of black suspense novels. His periods in Hollywood were a mixture of screenwriting, drinking and homosexual cruising. Jim Thompson was the author of tough guy novels, many of which have been filmed. He enjoys a higher reputation in France than in America or England. He worked in Los Angeles in the 1930s as a journalist and scriptwriter.

34. Browning is correct in respect of Marlene Dietrich and Billy Wilder, who were German-born. Paul Muni, however, was born in a part of Austria that was later incorporated into Poland, and Zimmerman was born in Vienna. Why Browning should have included Fred Astaire is unclear. Perhaps his aversion to *Top Hat* is responsible. Astaire's real name was Austerlitz, which is a place in Czechoslovakia. Geography, presumably, was not a subject at which Browning scintillated at Dudleigh Grammar.

35. There is no record of Johnny Weismuller performing such a feat. Perhaps Browning simply thought it would be a good stunt.

36. See Appendix.

37. Mushy Callahan (Vincent Morris Scheer) was junior welterweight champion of the world, 1926-30. He worked in Hollywood for many years preparing actors such as Flynn, Kirk Douglas and Elvis Presley for their roles in boxing pictures. Jimmy Sharman was a showman who toured Australian cities and country towns for many years with a boxing troupe. See my *Lords of the Ring: a history of prizefighting in Australia,* (Sydney, 1980), chap. 9.

38. Anthony Quinn, *The Original Sin,* (New York, 1972), chap. 17; Cecil B. De Mille, *Autobiography,* (New York, 1959), pp. 349–53.

ALSO BY PETER CORRIS

The 'Browning' Series
'Box Office' Browning

Richard Browning is a crack-shot, six-foot, all-Australian ex-private-school horseman. He is determined to con his way into the new world of film-making, but his way to Hollywood is thwarted by World War One, a series of unfortunate affairs and a disastrous marriage. In his developing career as box office poison, Browning makes far more enemies than movies.

'Box Office' Browning is Browning's recollection of his early days from an ungraceful old age. The truth may be filtered through booze, drugs and a lot of years, but the escapades with the famous and infamous are a delight.

'Beverly Hills' Browning

Richard Browning has a marvellous taste for mucking up even lucky breaks. In fact, he's only really good at one thing; that is, getting away.

Sure, the would-be Aussie movie star makes it to the U.S. of A., but San Francisco proves to be a long way from the starlets, palm trees and swimming pools of Hollywood, at least by the route only he could choose, through Mexico. And then, when he gets to Beverly Hills, he finds bootleggers in the swimming pools, anarchists on the movie sets and starlets just too hot to handle. Not to mention making an enemy of the 'king' of Hollywood, Douglas Fairbanks – the 'city of dreams' becomes nightmare land.

Browning Takes Off

After being coerced into doing time in the Royal Canadian Mounted Police, Richard Kelly Browning decides the Mountie life is not for him and escapes via the Yukon and Chicago.

Joining forces with compatriot Bluey Tait, he learns to fly and the two of them are contracted to work for Howard Hughes on his multimillion dollar blockbuster, *Hell's Angels*. The Hollywood life is more Dick's scene and life seems sweet for a while. But his past is just behind a palm tree and threatening to engulf him . . .

The Pokerface Series
Pokerface
In this thriller the player with the best pokerface wins the game – and it's a dangerous game. Sacked from the shadowy Federal Security Agency, his marriage tottering, Ray Crawley forms an association with radical punk Roxy and her friends – and that's his first mistake.

Crawley's former boss Toby Campion is trying to manipulate him in a game with Canberra. But Crawley is still in the game, and he won't give up. All the players are holding good cards but will the best hand win?

The Baltic Business
'There was a bomb scare,' Crawley said. 'Probably a hoax but whose hoax? They're a weird lot, I can tell you.'

A routine assignment draws Crawley into a web of murder and intrigue involving Eastern European refugees marked by the dark days of the DP camps. His marriage assumes a new dimension as Mandy takes to university study and he takes to the lovely Irina Gilbus whose father heads a shadowy organization known as Nations in Chains.

Set in Melbourne, Peter Corris' thriller features hard-boiled secret-service man Ray Crawley and his old mate Huck, the stars of *Pokerface*.

The Kimberley Killing
A routine blood test after a car accident involving a retired Attorney General starts Ray 'Creepy' Crawley and offsider Huck in their latest investigation.

They need to delve into the gay sub-culture, though Crawley finds the young widow, Christine Kimberley, far more interesting. The trail moves from Melbourne to Sydney to the Barossa Valley as Crawley and Huck realise they are dealing with some very powerful forces beyond Australia.

The Cargo Club
After a quiet time in Canberra, Crawley is sent to Vitatavu to discredit a government Minister. He becomes involved in the political struggle for control of the island when he is taken hostage by the MMU guerrillas. His old mate Huck comes to the rescue but will he be in time . . .